RETRIBUTION

HARRY WATERMAN

Retribution

My sincere thanks for their invaluable advice and time to:

Doug Galloway
Chris Sheppard
Watermark Publications

The Embassy of the Islamic Republic of Iran, London, early April

Gilgamesh Jazani, the Iranian ambassador to London,

had originally refused to see Jamal Karam, but her persistence had paid off and one morning in early April their paths had crossed outside the embassy. Seeing the beautiful woman approach him, insisting that she had: *"Extremely important information concerning the economic welfare of Iran!"* the ambassador succumbed and invited her into the embassy.

Standing behind his large, leather-topped desk, dressed in a black, pinstriped suit, Jazani regarded the alluring woman facing him; she was wearing a black hijab and a black dress. Her olive complexion was near flawless and her dark, sultry eyes were intoxicating and tantalisingly irresistible. Her bright-red lips were the only outward sign of her rebellious nature.

'Please, take a seat,' he said as he lit a cigarette. 'I must say Miss Karam, if nothing else, you are a very *persistent* woman.'

'Oh—there's a lot more to me than that, Mister Ambassador,' she replied confidently, as she settled on one of a pair of ornate, brushed-silk sofas that were separated by a low, marble-topped table.

Gilgamesh Jazani's face was full and plump and the wisps of black hair that remained on his head were oiled and combed straight back. His gold-rimmed glasses were far too big for his face and a well-trimmed, moustache adorned his top lip.

'I have ordered some tea and cake, it will be arriving shortly,' he said, with an insipid grin that exposed his smoke-stained teeth and gold fillings.

Jamal smiled and replied politely:

'How nice of you, Ambassador.'

With a condescending tone he asked:

'So… what is it that *you* have that could possibly affect the economic welfare of *my* country?'

With that there was a knock on the office door and a young woman, wearing a sand-coloured hijab and full-length black dress, walked in carrying a tray of Persian tea and Yazdi cakes (cup cakes). The ambassador gestured to her, in a condescending way, to leave the tray on the marble table. The woman subserviently obliged and smiled weakly at Jamal before leaving the office without a word being spoken.

Jamal smiled as the familiar smell of cardamon filled her nostrils.

'I love them but sadly they're not good for my waistline,' the ambassador said, tapping his rotund tummy.

There was something about him that she didn't like, but business was business, she quickly reminded herself.

The ambassador walked over to the table. 'Sugar?' he asked, as he poured tea into two fine-china teacups.

'One lump please,' she said, and took the steaming cup offered to her. She watched her host settle on the sofa opposite her and excitedly inspect the tray of colourful cakes, before finally forcing a whole one into his mouth.

'Help yourself,' he mumbled.

Jamal smiled and ignored his offer. '…To answer your question, sir—I have something for you that will, without doubt,' Jamal leaned forward for effect and looked deep into his eyes, 'persuade the Americans to unconditionally *remove* much of the trade embargo on your country; and that, I'm sure you will agree, would be worth *billions* of dollars to Iran?'

The next cupcake the ambassador was about to devour never reached his mouth. '… Are you a mad woman?' he snarled.

'Do I look like a mad woman, Ambassador?' Jamal replied, coolly.

'…There is *nothing* you have young lady, that would persuade the Americans to do such a thing—so please—do not waste my time any further.'

Jamal leaned forward, took a cupcake and devoured it sensuously. '…Mmmm, delicious,' she said, seductively wiping the sides of her mouth with her index finger. 'We have similar cakes in Syria ,' she concluded with a wry smile.

The ambassador began to stand.

Jamal quickly added:

'I guarantee you there is *something* I have Mister Ambassador, and it's for sale to you at a cost of *thirty-million US dollars;* an absolute bargain, even if I say so myself, and the quickest return on investment Iran will ever have offered to them on a plate.'

The ambassador scoffed:

'… W*hat on* earth are *you* selling that's worth *thirty-million dollars!* Miss Karam?'

Jamal giggled. '…I'm selling the best poker hand Iran could ever be dealt; a hand that will make Iran a *respected* player on the world stage, instead of a struggling, volatile country *crippled* by antiquated, religious bigots and sweeping economic sanctions.'

The ambassador closed his eyes and huffed in despair. 'You are mad and downright rude, and you have wasted enough of my valuable time. You have accepted my hospitality and in return you have chosen to insult the *great* Republic of Iran.' Gilgamesh Jazani gestured to the door. 'Would you now please leave.'

'I only speak the truth,' Jamal replied. 'Please, let me explain. I'm offering Iran t*op-secret* Russian military information, Ambassador; *information* that the Americans would lick your arse and suck your cock for!'

Her host stiffened and blushed with embarrassment at her vulgar comment but Jamal Karam never took her eyes off him.

'...You have *five* minutes, young lady,' he said, 'to tell me exactly what *kind* of information you're selling.'

Jamal continued, knowing she had his undivided attention.

'...I'm offering Iran top-secret information about the location of *numerous* hidden underground missile, bomb and chemical warfare sites in Russia. The kind of armaments being manufactured and the throughput at each of the sites. Also, *detailed* information about the whereabouts of storage facilities for both conventional and nuclear weapons and—if that's not enough—four locations of major cyber centres that the Russians are developing to wreak havoc on the West's financial infrastructures, together with two sites where Russia is developing genetic engineering tools to manipulate human DNA.'

The ambassador sneered. 'How could *you* possibly know all of this?'

'Simple,' Jamal replied, 'I have access to *genuine* inside information.'

'I'm sorry young lady but I don't believe you.'

Jamal smirked and then stood up. 'But the Americans will,' she said, as she walked towards the door. 'They have suspected Russia of lying for some time, and now that Russia has pulled out of the Intermediate-Range Nuclear Forces Treaty, Iran could offer the Americans *concrete* evidence to support their claims. Russia would be stripped naked in front of the whole world with nowhere to hide its filthy modesty. A massive negotiating chip, wouldn't you agree?'

'Do you expect me to believe that you would sell that information to the *Americans?—A*fter what they did to *your* country!'

Jamal stopped and slowly turned around. 'Bashar al-Assad, Putin, Trump, Saddam Hussain, ISIS, it's the same power game and sadly, *innocent* people always get killed as part of that game. And frankly for thirty-million dollars, Ambassador, I would sell my *mother* to the Americans!' Jamal then walked to the door and reached for the handle. 'Thank you for your time and the delicious Yazdi cakes.'

'…Please!—Wait a moment!' he called out, in a conciliatory tone—'We need to talk. Please—come back and sit down.'

Jamal fought back a smile and returned to her seat on the sofa. She watched the ambassador light another cigarette; he inhaled deeply and then, looking into Jamal's eyes, he said:

'You know that extremely sensitive military information of this nature can get you killed, don't you?'

'Are *you* threatening me, Ambassador?'

'Oh no—certainly not, young lady! I was thinking more like —Mister Putin, for example.'

Jamal replied resolutely:

'I'll take my chances, Mister Ambassador.'

She then watched as a pensive Gilgamesh Jazani got to his feet, walked over to his desk and picked up the telephone handset. After a momentary pause he said in Persian:

'...Put me through to Tehran.'

Retribution

RETRIBUTION

retribution | rɛtrɪˈbjuːʃ(ə)n |

(noun)

punishment inflicted on someone as vengeance for a wrong or criminal act:

Retribution

Chapter 1

GET YOUR COAT GIRL

Probe's Offices, Cambridge, 11.30 am, Monday 6 May

When Alan Cornish walked into his office his desk phone was ringing.

Tapping the flashing button, he said:

'Yes, Rachel?'

'Alan, I have a Chief Superintendent Montgomery from Scotland Yard on the line. He says he needs to speak with you urgently.'

That's the new boy, Cornish thought. 'Put him through, please, Rachel,' Cornish replied, as he settled into his captain's chair…

'You're through,' the receptionist replied.

'…Chief Superintendent—this is Alan Cornish speaking—What can I do for you, sir?'

'Ah, yes,' came the reply, 'thank you for taking my call, Mister Cornish.'

'Please—call me Alan. My secretary said it was urgent—so what exactly is it about?'

'… I have a double murder on the books and to tell you the truth my department is sinking fast under the current workload. Between you and me, I simply don't have enough officers. I've been advised to contact your organisation for assistance in solving this—double murder.'

'So what are the circumstances, sir?'

'The victims are a young Russian artist by the name of Maksim Mikhailov and his girlfriend. Their bodies were found in his Soho apartment by their cleaning lady this morning… Both of them had been *decapitated!'*

'Oh dear!'

'The girl was killed whilst tied to a chair in the middle of the room and the man was decapitated in the bath.'

'Not your average murder!'

'Exactly! But this is London, Alan—not bloody Iraq! And I can't hold off the press for much longer, I'm afraid. So it's going to be a *low* profile, botched robbery, murder investigation. Two foreigners, decapitated in our *civilised*, capital city! Can you imagine what would happen if the press got their hands on this? The information we feed them needs to be carefully managed and there must be *absolutely* no mention of the decapitations, otherwise they're going to have a fucking field day! I want Probe to take on the case, Alan.'

'…When did this happen, sir?'

'The bodies were discovered at nine-thirty this morning; we're waiting for forensics to pinpoint the time of death more accurately. I've already briefed Ronnie Jarvis, who I believe you already know, that I intend to use your services for this case.'

'And will we be given full investigative powers?'

'Absolutely you will! Open access—what's ours is yours—and that includes access to GCHQ. It's your call! The Russian had a legitimate passport and I'm informed that he was recently granted political asylum here.'

Political asylum—for an artist? Cornish mused.

'But the girl is so far unidentified—all we know about her is that she's not caucasian.'

'Okay, sir, when do you need an answer?'

'I need a *positive* answer now! Your organisation, Alan, has the resources and the expertise to take this one on. Obviously we will pay your *extortionate* rates in the hope that the whole, nasty incident will be resolved in the very near future and in the most discreet way possible.'

'Not knowing the case details, sir, it's difficult for me to comment on how long it might take.'

'I realise that, Alan, but I'm sure you understand that I don't have an unlimited budget.'

'I appreciate that sir.' Cornish, unusually, made a 'snap' decision. '…I'll get the paperwork set up and we'll get the show on the road ASAP, sir.'

'Good man! Thank you for your cooperation. The powers-that-be are insisting that this case be solved *very* quickly…so please don't let me down. And on that note, Alan, Ronnie Jarvis is expecting you at the crime scene in Broadwick Street at three o'clock this afternoon for a handover meeting!'

Cornish grinned and glanced at his watch. *Clearly this guy was not going to take no for an answer.* 'Yes, I've worked with Ronnie before, sir… Rest assured, I'll be there.'

'Excellent, and good luck.'

'Thank you.' Cornish replaced the handset and leaned back in his chair. 'Double decapitation,' he said, pensively. With that there was a knock on his door. 'Come in,' he called out, and smiled when Melanie Underwood entered.

'Get your coat, girl,' he said, 'we have an appointment in town.'

'But…'

'No buts—double murder—high priority.'

'Oh—that sounds nasty.'

'It is. Double decapitation!'

'Oh my god!' Melanie raised her hand to her mouth.

'Are you up for it?'

Melanie paused, thinking about the implications. '…Yes,' she said, stiffening.

'Are you sure?'

'…I can't honestly say I'm sure, but I suppose it comes with the territory doesn't it?'

'I'm afraid it does, my love.'

Melanie took a deep breath. 'It's not something you'd expect to happen in London is it?'

Cornish raised his eyebrows. 'That's exactly what the authorities are saying and they want it hushed up. If the press get their hands on this *we'll* be *beheaded* in the Tower of London.'

Chapter 2

PUTTING ON A BRAVE FACE

Cornish and Melanie turned right, off Poland Street, and walked up Broadwick Street towards the address blinking on the screen of her iPhone. They didn't notice the man standing on the opposite corner, taking discreet photographs of them on his phone as they passed by him.

Outside the front door of the four-story building, a uniformed officer watched with interest as Cornish and Melanie approached. Melanie was dressed in a charcoal grey, pinstripe jacket, matching skirt and white blouse as she strode confidently towards him; the officer never really noticed Cornish. The weather was getting unusually warm for May but she'd resisted the urge to remove her jacket; aware the young officer, standing outside the front door of the crime scene, was already transfixed on her gently swaying breasts.

As she approached him she said:

'Good afternoon, officer, I'm Melanie Underwood and this is Alan Cornish, we're from *Probe*. SIO Ronnie Jarvis is expecting us?'

Only then did the officer look up at Melanie's face. 'Can I see your IDs please?' he asked.

Melanie showed him her ID card first, followed by Cornish, at which the officer waved them through. 'Second floor,' he said, opening the front door for them. 'I hope you're not too squeamish,' he added, as they walked past him; his eyes were now firmly fixed on Melanie's pert bottom.

Putting on a brave face she followed Cornish up the stairs, with legs that suddenly felt like jelly.

The police officer squeezed the growing lump in his groin. 'Get down you beast,' he whispered to himself.

The entrance to the apartment was guarded by another uniformed officer, who also requested to see their IDs. They obliged, then it took them a few moments, to the amusement of the officer, to don their all-in-one white, forensic suits, elasticated plastic shoe covers, latex gloves and elasticated caps. Finally, he opened the front door for them to enter the apartment.

Cornish turned to Melanie. 'If it gets too much for you, go down into the street and get some fresh air—okay?'

Melanie took a deep breath. 'Okay,' she said, trying to compose herself.

As they entered the apartment they could immediately smell blood; it was infused into the unusually warm, stagnant air in the room. In front of them, tied to a chair in the middle of a blood-stained carpet, a headless female body was slumped towards them; her tee-shirt and jeans were soaked in blood. On the carpet some three feet to the right of the chair lay the victim's head. A tangled, bloody mess of raven-black hair partly covered her pallid face and her cold eyes seemed to stare upwards in disbelief as the three-man forensics team busied themselves, taking photographs and swabbing the place for prints.

Oh my God!—I'm not sure I can do this, Melanie thought, desperately trying to steady herself. She quickly realised she was outside of her comfort zone.

'Are you okay, ma'am?' the officer asked from outside the door.

'…Yes—yes, thank you officer, I'm okay,' she replied, rather unconvincingly; at the same time trying desperately to hold down the contents of her stomach.

Cornish turned to Melanie and began to say:

'Do you want—'

'You won't be able to use the bathroom I'm afraid,' interrupted Ronnie Jarvis, as he strode out of a door to their left. 'Thanks for coming,' he said, and shook hands with Cornish. 'It's like a waxworks horror show in here. Are you all right, girl?' he asked the ashen-faced Melanie wavering next to Cornish.

'I'll be okay in a moment,' she replied, looking up to the ceiling. She grabbed Cornish's arm before taking a few deep breaths.

'Take a look at this,' Jarvis said, excitedly, leading Cornish off to the bathroom.

Melanie walked over to one of two armchairs next to a window table and as she sat down she clumsily knocked an Amazon box off the table onto the floor. She picked it up to replace it and noticed that the bottom and the back of the box had been cut away, but she thought nothing more of it. She closed her eyes and took a few deep breaths. 'There's no way I could have prepared myself for this,' she said, quietly to herself.

Against her better judgement, but strangely compelled, she glanced over at the girl's severed head for a brief moment and then quickly turned her gaze out of the window, as if to wipe the gruesome image from her mind. *How could anyone do that to another human being?*

Jarvis opened the bathroom door and Cornish looked in. In front of him, in the large bath, the decapitated body of a man lay partly submerged in blood-red water. To the right, on the floor near the toilet, his pallid, wax-like head lay on its side.

'Take a look at his head—what's left of it that is,' Jarvis said to Cornish.

Cornish entered the bathroom and knelt down to take a closer look. 'Shot in the forehead,' he said.

'Yeah, they blew his brains out. He was shot in the head *and* then decapitated!'

Looking at the wall behind the bath and pointing to the blood splattered tiles, Cornish said;

'So he was shot in the bath.'

'Yeah—that's what's left of his brains all right... Melanie, you need to see this,' Jarvis called out.

Melanie walked tentatively towards the bathroom door. *Shit! Don't be sick now—take deep breaths girl—deep breaths.* The first thing she saw was the Russian's head with its gaping mouth and the neat bullet hole between his eyes. Cornish raised his arm to block her entrance as she approached the door and said:

'I think you've seen enough for one day, don't you?'

Melanie turned and rushed to the front door.

One hour later, Cornish, Melanie and Jarvis were sitting in the pub on the opposite side of Broadwick Street. Melanie was drinking her second, double whisky and a healthy, pink glow had returned to her cheeks.

'I thought I was ready, but I wasn't,' she said. '—I was sick all over the police officer's boots for God's sake!'

Cornish bit his lip and fought hard to stop himself from laughing. Jarvis got up and walked out under the pretext of wanting a smoke.

'...It's never easy, my love,' Cornish said, and put his arm around her.

'I feel so bloody stupid, Alan,' Melanie said, and began to sob.

'You're not the first—and you certainly won't be the last to be affected by such scenes. It's my fault—I shouldn't have sent you in there.'

'No!...It's *not* your fault!'Melanie insisted, 'It's all part of the job and it's something I have to come to terms with.' Melanie blew her nose into a tissue. 'It was the smell that got to me first Alan; that warm, *acrid* smell.' Melanie took a deep breath and tried to compose herself. 'The pain that poor girl must have suffered—it's fucking *barbaric* what they did to them!...I'll be more prepared next time—I promise... I'll have the whisky first,' she said, and allowed herself a nervous giggle.

Cornish empathised and kissed her forehead. 'Another one?'

'No—*definitely* no more, thank you. This is quite enough.'

Cornish smiled sympathetically and walked to the bar and ordered another two pints of Doom Bar, knowing Jarvis wouldn't refuse another drink. When he returned he placed the pints on the table and sat down next to Melanie again. 'Was it worth it?' he asked.

Melanie looked at him. 'Me, going in *there* you mean?'

'Yeah.'

'Oh yes—most definitely, unless of course you're the police officer! He might not agree with me,' Melanie replied, resting her head on Cornish's shoulder. 'You know what they say, what doesn't kill you—'

'Makes you stronger,' Cornish added. *I love you, girl*, he thought.

Melanie sighed. '…He was clearly a very talented surrealist painter that young Russian, but he definitely wasn't a fan of Vladimir Putin or the Russian regime! His paintings in the apartment are quite graphic and they seem to be mocking modern Russian society. Did you see the painting of a Russian military tank hovering over a deep pit?'

'Yes, I did,' replied Cornish.

'Half of the tank was made of red butterflies. One side of the pit was barren and scorched and on the butterfly side it was green and people were climbing up the vegetation and escaping from the pit.'

Cornish sipped his beer pensively for a moment, thinking about Melanie's words, and then he said:

'I'm amazed you noticed such detail my love—under the circumstances I mean.'

Melanie smiled through tight lips and said:

'I think the adrenalin rush elevated my senses to a level I never realised was possible.'

Cornish continued:

'I've seen some of his work on my phone. I think he was a bit of a rebel, don't you? His work reminds me of a modern day Dante; dark and depressing.'

Melanie sat upright. 'Maybe Russia was his Hell! Do you think he was silenced by the Russians?'

'Most likely—but the *decapitation*? That was something the seventeenth century Romanovs might have done, but it's definitely not Putin's style.'

'No, I agree,' Melanie added.

Cornish downed the remains of his pint. 'Why would you shoot someone in the head and then cut their head off after they're dead? It doesn't make any sense.'

Melanie shivered.

'Do you feel up to visiting one of the galleries that's exhibiting Mikhailov's work?' Cornish asked.

Melanie nodded and said:

'Yeah—let's do it!'

'According to my phone, the Pace Gallery is only a ten-minute walk from here—but before that, I need to visit his apartment again. How do you feel about going back there with me?'

Melanie finished her whiskey in one and said:

'…Yes,…I'll be okay this time. I know what to expect now.'

Cornish smiled and hugged her. 'That's my girl,' he enthused, knowing it was important for her to face the scene again, and sooner rather than later.

Jarvis walked back into the pub and smiled when he saw the fresh pint on the table. 'Cheers mate,' he said. 'I need to officially handover the case to you guys, so you'll need to come to my office asap.'

Cornish replied:

'I bet you're happy to hand this one over aren't you Ronnie?'

'Rather you than me,' he answered, before taking a large sip of his beer.

'It's love-you-and-leave-you I'm afraid, Ronnie,' Cornish said, as he stood up. 'We're off to the Pace Gallery to see what we can learn about the Russian.'

'Good luck,' Jarvis said, happy to stay put and enjoy his pint.

It was another hour before Melanie and Cornish walked into the brightly lit art gallery, in Burlington Gardens.

A female security guard acknowledged them and Cornish walked over to her.

'Who's in charge here?' he asked.

'What's it concerning, sir?'

'We need some information about an artist.'

'Which particular artist would that be, sir?'

'Maksim Mikhailov,' Cornish replied.

'Please wait here,' the female guard said and walked off. A few moments later she returned with a tall, elegant woman who was dressed in a dark trouser suit and cream blouse. She greeted them with a broad smile and said:

'Good evening both; my name's Claudia, I'm the Curatorial Assistant here. I understand you're interested in the work of Maksim Mikhailov, is that right?'

Cornish smiled and replied:

'We're more interested in the person than in his work.'

The curator frowned. 'I'm sorry—I don't understand.'

'My name's Alan Cornish and this is my colleague, Melanie Underwood,' he responded, as they both showed the assistant their ID badges. 'We're private investigators, currently working for the Metropolitan Police. We'd like to ask you a few questions about Maksim Mikhailov.'

The curator visibly tensed. 'Is Max in some kind of trouble?' she asked.

'How well do you know him?' Melanie enquired.

'…Quite well. We're currently exhibiting eight of his oils. He's all the rage at the moment; especially in the Middle East.'

'The Middle East? Why is that?' Cornish asked.

'A lot of very wealthy collectors… I'm afraid the art world is a very fickle place Mr Cornish; one day your work is fashionable, the next day somebody else's work is all the rage —unless you're Picasso, Van Gogh or Monet of course. Let's just say Max is very popular at the moment. We've sold three of his works in the last month, and they're not exactly cheap! He told me that he had also recently finished a commission of *ten* oil paintings for an undisclosed buyer… so… what exactly do you want to know about him?'

Cornish responded:

'I presume you are someone that has an in-depth knowledge of the art world?'

'Yes—I'd like to think so.'

'Would you say that Mikhailov's work warranted such high prices, Miss Hall?'

The curator huffed 'The buyer ultimately decides what the value of the artist's work will be, Mr Cornish.'

'But—in your opinion?'

'…As I said, the *buyer* ultimately decides.'

'Yes, of course'…Cornish looked around. 'Is there somewhere where we can talk in private, Claudia?'

The curator once again frowned at the request. 'Yes,—there is—follow me please.' The assistant led them off to a small meeting room to the right of the main entrance.

All three settled on chairs around a small table and then Cornish said:

'Thank you, Claudia. We need to know more about Maksim Mikhailov.'

'So he is in trouble then?'

Cornish glanced at Melanie and then looked back at the assistant. 'What can you tell us about him? For instance, when was the last time you saw him?'

The assistant answered immediately:

'Saturday night; we were at a party in Kensington. He was there with Jamal.'

'Jamal?'

'Yes—his girlfriend.'

'What can you tell us about Jamal?' Melanie asked.

'Not a lot really; she's a real beauty though and full of life. She's madly in love with Max and I think they're planning to get married at some time in the future. I believe she works for an up-market employment agency somewhere in town.'

'How long has she been with Maksim?'

Claudia tensed. 'What's all this about?'

'Please—answer the question, Claudia,' Melanie insisted.

17

Claudia let out a sigh. '...Ever since *I've* known them—which must be—two years.'

'So her name is Jamal?—Jamal what?' Melanie asked.

'...I don't know... I only know her as Jamal.'

'Do you know where she lives?' Cornish asked.

'I think she lives with him, now that he's moved into his new apartment, but I'm not sure. I don't understand; why don't you just ask them yourselves?'

Cornish glanced at Melanie again.

'Has something happened to them?' The curator suddenly became agitated. 'They are all right aren't they?'

Melanie glanced at Cornish and he nodded.

'I'm sorry to have to tell you this, but they're both dead,' she said. '...There was a robbery at their apartment and they were killed by the intruders.'

Claudia raised her hands to her face. 'Oh my God!' she exclaimed.

Chapter 3

IT'S ALL YOURS MATE

Ronnie Jarvis flopped into his office chair. 'It appears that Probe's success has reached the very top at the Yard,' he said in a monotone voice, gesturing to Alan Cornish to take a seat in front of his cluttered desk.

When Cornish had settled, Jarvis asked:

'Coffee? Because I can't think without one.'

Cornish smiled and replied:

'I know the feeling!—White with, please, Ronnie.'

A few moments later, Jarvis returned with two steaming mugs and settled back into his chair behind his desk. Leaning forward he handed a mug to Cornish. 'I think that's the one with sugar.'

'Thanks,' Cornish replied. Taking the steaming mug by the handle he could smell the smoke on Jarvis's breath.

'Just look at this lot,' Jarvis whinged despondently, pointing to the heap of case files on both sides of his desk. 'How the hell is one man supposed to do an efficient day's work when the workload just keeps coming in? I've never known it this bad, in all of the years I've been on the force.'

'I guess that's why they called us in, Ronnie.'

'Yeah, I guess so,' he said, before taking a sip of coffee from his mug. 'They clearly have no problem spending money on you, but when I ask for some, they suddenly don't have any. That, Alan, really *pisses* me off!'

Cornish smiled sympathetically. 'Nothing changes, mate.'

Jarvis continued:

'No—you're right… This must be my tenth cup of coffee today! Do you know what? Sometimes I *fucking detest* this job!'

Cornish sipped his coffee as he regarded a very despondent Jarvis. *He's looking older,* he thought, remembering back to the police conferences they'd both attended over the years. He still had his trademark fake tan and once pioneering bleached teeth (which he achieved using a watered down solution of *Domestos*)! But time, or stress, or cigarettes, or the combination of all of them was beginning to catch up with him now and the wrinkles around his eyes and on his neck were sadly betraying this Oscar Wilde's Dorian Gray-like, character.

Cornish said:

'Melanie really enthused about the lovely lunch she had with you,'

Jarvis looked somewhat surprised by the comment. 'Did she?' he asked.

'Yeah! Well, it's not often you get treated to lunch and champagne at the Waldorf, is it?'

Ronnie Jarvis's mouth dropped open. 'She told you that?'

'Ronnie—how you operate is your own business.'

'…Yeah—that's right… Don't get the wrong idea though… I wasn't coming on to her.'

'I wasn't suggesting you were, Ronnie.' Cornish struggled to keep a straight face.

Jarvis had clearly tensed. 'Anyway, she'd already told me that you two were—*lovers*. She's a bit tasty, ain't she?—You *lucky* bastard!'

Cornish smiled. 'Yeah—I guess I am. But I still find it hard to believe that she wants *me*.'

Jarvis ran his fingers through his hair and said:

'I know exactly what you mean, Alan. You'd think a fit little thing like that would want a virile, young stud, wouldn't you? Not a burnt out old git like you!'

'Yeah, yeah,' Cornish replied.

Jarvis laughed. '…I trust she's fully recovered from her visit to the murder scene?'

'Yeah,' Cornish chuckled. 'I felt so sorry for her. She tried so hard to put on a brave face…'

'And then she puked all over PC Whitehouse's boots! It couldn't have happened to a nicer *twat!*' Jarvis laughed until a coughing fit took control of him. Eventually, regaining his composure, he said:

'I couldn't stick with one person. I need to uh—put it *about* a bit—if you know what I mean?'

'You haven't changed then?' Cornish replied.

After an embarrassing pause, Jarvis passed him a file. 'It's all yours mate.'

'Premeditated, without a doubt Ronnie—but messy. It doesn't feel like a professional job at all—apart from the bullet in the Russian's head.'

'My thoughts exactly,' Jarvis replied.

'Any more news on their identities?'

'We know he is twenty-four-year-old Maksim Mikhailov, from Moscow. Apparently he's been making a bit of a name for himself as an artist in town; hence the posh apartment. Melanie tells me the girl's name was Jamal and she was his girlfriend. She was obviously very attractive. I'd say she's Arab from the images, wouldn't you?'

'Perhaps; maybe Greek or Italian even.'

'Well, as there's no doubt we're paying you a king's ransom Alan—I'm hoping your organisation can enlighten this *overworked, underpaid* and totally *disgruntled* Senior Investigating Office on that very matter!'

Cornish grinned and nodded thoughtfully before replying:

'Together with enough evidence to convict whosoever it was that hacked their heads off, of course?'

Jarvis grinned through tight lips and replied:

'Oh yeah—that as well mate... Just don't expect much help from me, okay?'

'But you know, and I know, Ronnie, you wouldn't lose too much sleep if I failed with this one, would you?'

'...I can't deny that. But it's nothing personal you understand, Alan.'

Cornish nodded. 'When can we expect the full forensic report?'

'Not sure, but now this new guy, Montgomery, is involved, I suspect it'll be quite soon. I've sent out an email to all the interested parties informing them that Probe is now running the enquiry; so there's no need to ask my permission for anything.'

Cornish nodded and asked:

'What's going to happen once the press get hold of this?'

'What do you mean?'

Jarvis's computer pinged and he glanced at his monitor. 'Surprise, surprise, Alan—we're not releasing the gruesome decapitation details to the media. The official line is that it's a botched robbery and stabbings.'

'Yes, I know, but what about the cleaning lady—she witnessed the aftermath?' Cornish asked.

'Apparently, she's an illegal immigrant who speaks very little English. She's currently having trauma counselling. She won't be saying *anything* in public.'

'Do we have her statement?'

'Not yet—we're working on the translation.'

'Arabic?'

'Yeah,' replied Jarvis.

Cornish nodded. 'At this moment she has to be treated as a possible suspect. We'll start by checking the CCTV footage.'

'No stone to be left unturned, Alan.'

Cornish stood up and shook hands with Jarvis. 'Stay in touch,' he said.

'Yeah,' Jarvis replied, picking up his cigarette packet. 'I'll walk out with you, I need a smoke.'

'They're going to kill you!'

'Something's going to get me mate, might just as well be these fucking things.'

'Have you tried to give them up?'

'Nah!'

As they walked down the corridor towards the lifts, Jarvis stopped and looked at Cornish. 'Why would you shoot somebody in the head and then decapitate them afterwards?'

Cornish shook his head. 'That's a *very* good question Ronnie and one that intrigues me,' he replied, as they continued on.

Jarvis pressed the lift call button. 'There are too many *sick* fuckers out there, Alan,' he said, 'and I'm sorry to say but it's getting worse by the day… Are you going to take personal charge of this one, mate?' he asked as they entered the lift.

'…Yes, I am,' Cornish replied.

'I think this case is really going to test your investigative skills; and just like a boxer, you're only as good as your last fight!'

Cornish smiled and said:

'Thanks for those words of encouragement, Ronnie.'

Jarvis started to laugh and ended up having another coughing fit.

As the lift doors opened, Cornish said:

'Let's just hope you live long enough to see the result of my investigative skills!'

'I'd better, cos I've got myself a new filly and she can't keep her fucking hands off me.'

'Then I need to work quickly—in case she fucks you to death!' Cornish replied, with a wry smile

'What a way to go though!' Jarvis responded, with a broad, bleached-teeth smile.

In the foyer the two men shook hands again and Jarvis said:

'Good luck mate—you're going to need it.'

'So are you, by the sound of it!' replied Cornish, which triggered another of Jarvis' coughing fits!

Chapter 4

THE MEETING

Probe's Offices, Cambridge

Sitting around the meeting-room table were: Melanie Underwood, Zeezee and work colleagues Zac Monde, Alisha Berry and Tom Weiss. Zac Monde was a blonde haired, blue eyed, twenty-five-year-old with looks he inherited from his Swedish mother. He was an enthusiastic team member and a communications guru. Alisha Berry was a skinny twenty-eight-year-old Geordie with thick, brown hair cut in a bob, and she was an expert on Information Management. Tom Weiss was a tall, tough, middle-aged American with a crew cut and skin like leather. He'd worked as a detective on the streets of New York for nearly twenty years before joining Probe some five years earlier, looking for a new life and a new start, following the death of his wife after a hit-and-run incident whilst on holiday in Monterey, California.

'Okay,' Cornish began, 'now that we're all here, let's get started, guys... I'm sure that you've all heard the news about the recent botched robbery and double murder at Broadwick Street in London yesterday. That's the official line—but we all know the gruesome reality of it. This case is extremely embarrassing to the authorities and *we* have been tasked with finding the killer or killers. We are *officially* working for the Met, but in reality the case is under our control and I will be the SIO. The information we have at present is somewhat limited. We know the identity of the man; he's twenty-four-year-old artist, Maksim Mikhailov from Russia. The other victim was his girlfriend; currently, we know very little about her—other than her name is Jamal and that they planned to get married at some point in the future. Both of them were decapitated—but —Mikhailov was shot in the head, first and decapitated afterwards.'

Tom Weiss frowned. 'That's kinda odd, don't yer think? Why kill someone and then decapitate them afterwards?'

Cornish nodded. 'My thoughts exactly, Tom. So—we're looking for a person, or persons, who are extremely dangerous and most probably psychotic. Let's keep that in mind—at all times—throughout our investigations—because *your* safety is paramount!'

Cornish then continued:

'Alisha—I want you to manage all of the information we gather and produce all of the necessary visual stuff that you're so good at. This is going to be our operations and briefing room with regular progress meetings every two days; so the walls are all yours, my dear.'

Alisha smiled and nodded her approval.

'Zeezee and Zac, I want you both to check out the email, social media and phone communications of the victims for the last—say—six months, along with their banking details. The boys at the Met will give you all the assistance you need dealing with the phone companies; and get hold of the CCTV footage for a week before the murders.'

'Will do, boss,' Zac replied. Zeezee nodded.

'Tom—Do what you do best. Get out on the street and find their circle of friends. We need to know everything possible about the victims. Also interview their neighbours and the people living in the immediate area of the murder scene. Let's see what turns up.'

'Yes, sir,' replied Tom Weiss.

'Melanie I believe you're already investigating Jamal?'

Melanie nodded. 'Yes, I am. I'm chasing up a number of agencies in town to find where she worked and also if she has family here. If we knew where their phones were it would help, but they haven't turned up yet. It looks like the killers took them.'

Cornish replied:

'Okay stay with it. Now, I can't stress strongly enough that this investigation is of the highest priority and, as I said earlier, we will be working with the Met's resources, so let's all work together on this one and, if necessary, burn the midnight oil to bring to justice those responsible for this barbaric act. Good hunting everyone!'

*

East London, the previous March

'Sami! I've got another delivery for you,' the fat Turkish owner shouted from behind the counter.

The young, pizza delivery driver checked his phone's delivery app as he stood outside the takeaway smoking a cigarette. 'Yeah, I've got it, boss,' he said. 'This one will be my last delivery today, boss. I've got fings to do at the mosque tonight.'

'You and that bloody mosque! Why don't you get a life? A young kid like you should be out having fun, not down on his bloody knees all-day-long praying to Allah.'

The young Muslim picked up the food order from the counter and walked out of the takeaway to his work's scooter and slipped on his crash helmet. Before setting off into the London traffic he looked back into the shop and waved to his boss. 'You fat non-believer! One day you will suffer the pain that you deserve, because it is the will of Allah... Allahu Akbar!'

*

Charles Bridge, Prague—Early April

The young man standing on the famous bridge was looking down at the Vltava River; the cold mass of water below him moved steadily, deliberately, occasionally reflecting the weak sun which had appeared through the early morning mist. To his left, elevated above the mist, the ninth century Prague Castle and St Vitus Cathedral stood majestic, bathed in the golden, early morning sunshine.

From a pocket of his overcoat, the young man took out a packet of Marlboro and a Zippo and lit a cigarette, inhaling the smoke deep into his lungs. He turned his head slowly to his right and watched as another, older man, approached. The older man stopped next to him and peered over the side of the bridge at the river. He then looked up at the stone figures next to them on the balustrade.'May I speak English?' he asked.

'Russian, English, Czech, French, Italian, take your pick,' the young man replied, blowing smoke into the cold morning air.

'Impressive,' he said, who is it?

'Francis Xavier,' the young man replied, remembering his instructions. 'It's by Ferdinand Brokoff.'

The older man forced a weak smile before reaching into his coat and pulling out a plain, brown envelope. 'It contains a USB stick and twenty-five-thousand US dollars, as agreed; another fifty-thousand will be paid to you in dollars after the job is successfully completed.'

The younger man, took the envelope and tossed his cigarette into the river. 'It's good to do business with you again,' he said, and strode off in the direction of Wenceslas Square. The older man watched him for a few moments as he strode purposefully away. Then, taking out his mobile phone he made a call:

'…Он доставлен,' (it's delivered) he said in Russian, and walked off in the direction of the castle.

Twenty minutes later the younger man was sitting in a cafe in Wenceslas Square. He sipped his coffee and then plugged the USB stick into his laptop. Moments later he was reading a set of instructions and viewing photographs of his intended victim.

'Maksim Mikhailov,' he said, quietly. 'What have you been doing, you bad Russian boy?' *Something very serious, no doubt, because they want you dead,* he thought. In Tomas Soukal's mind, Mikhailov was simply another pay cheque. He did not see his victims as human beings, or feel any kind of remorse after he'd killed them. In fact, Tomas Soukal was the perfect assassin: he was a highly intelligent, disciplined and well-organised killing machine. Born in Brno in the Czech Republic, the twenty-eight-year-old started killing professionally when he was twenty-two, and now he was one of three top assassins operating in Europe. Even though he hated the Russians for invading his homeland, he was happy to take their money for the second time in three years. This job would be his tenth professional kill and take his total earnings to over four-hundred-thousand euros; impressive, when you consider his mother died in childbirth and his penniless, alcoholic father died when he was just a scrawny, twelve-year-old street-kid. But, even at that young age, he was already an expert at killing and eating almost anything simply out of necessity; especially after he'd been orphaned; it was simply a matter of survival of the fittest.

After the death of his father, he'd taught himself to read and write and he'd earned money slaughtering pigs and organising boar-hunting trips for foreign visitors. It was on those hunting trips that he'd realised he had a natural propensity for languages.

But, ten years later, he'd discovered that slaughtering *humans* was *far* more profitable. His memories of his first kill were still vivid in his mind; he could smell the Dutch informer's urine that had puddled on the floor, seconds before he'd nervously fired six rounds into the back of his head—which had exploded like a melon. He remembered having to wait for the silencer to cool down before he could unscrew it and the shards of bone that had stuck to the bottom of his jeans and the Dutchman's bulbous eye on the carpet; indelible memories.

Later that inaugural night, Tomas Soukal had paid for the pleasure of two prostitutes, smoked sixteen Marlboro Red cigarettes and downed a bottle and a half of expensive Polish vodka—before finally passing out, naked and spent, on the carpet of his hotel room.

His next kill—eight months later—had been a lot less stressful.

The young assassin checked his Rolex, closed his laptop and downed his espresso. He had a tram to catch and a busy schedule to organise; a professional kill took a lot of careful planning and he had a reputation to protect. He'd decided he was going to drive to the UK and take his Glock with him. The secret compartment he'd had fitted to his new S-Class Mercedes was about to be put to the test.

Chapter 5

WIMPOLE STREET

Probe's Offices

It was about 09.30 when the call came in from Scotland Yard. Melanie took it and was put through to the clearly distressed owner of the Lotus Employment Agency, calling to say he'd heard the terrible news about the murders and wanted to know if there was anything he could do to help. Within twenty minutes Melanie was on the train heading towards Wimpole Street in London.

'Melanie Underwood—Criminal Psychologist—Probe— Private Investigation Services,' Michael Adisa said, reading from the calling card that looked so small balanced between his fingers.

'So why aren't the police investigating this?' he asked, offering Melanie a mug of coffee. The tall, black, African owner of the agency towered over her, like a giant block of ebony as she gazed up at him from her chair. With his shaven head and smooth skin, Melanie struggled to guess his age. *Anywhere between thirty and fifty* she estimated.

'Thank you,' she said, taking the steaming mug offered to her. 'To answer your question, we are working on *behalf* of the Metropolitan Police on this case. They use our services quite often, depending on their workload,' Melanie explained. 'We offer specialist services that they often don't have because of resource problems… So you say Jamal had worked for you for over two years?'

The big African nodded. 'Yes, for nearly three now; I can't believe it's been that long. I can't *believe* she's dead,' he said, solemnly. 'When I heard the news about the murdered Russian I realised that it was Jamal that had been killed too.'

'Does she have family in London?'

'I think she has a brother, but they didn't get on, from what I can gather.'

Melanie frowned.

'Jamal was a Muslim you see, but she relinquished her faith, and her brother, who is apparently a *devout* Muslim, disowned her.'

'Oh, I see.' *That sounds suspicious,* she thought.

'She was from Syria but her family all died in the war, apart from her brother that is.'

'Do you know where I can find him?'

'I have no idea, I'm sorry…She was planning on marrying her artist boyfriend you know.'

Melanie smiled weakly. 'Yes, I know. It's all very sad. Was she living with him?'

'I believe she'd moved in with him, yes.'

'Do you have her old address?'

'We must have it on record. I'll make sure you have it before you leave.'

'Thank you. There doesn't seem to be any trace of her passport or mobile. Do you keep that information on record?'

'Yes, I'm sure we must do,' Michael Adisa raised his eyebrows, 'if she had a passport, that is—coming from Syria!'

'If you do have her details it would be a great help, Mr Adisa.'

The big African smiled broadly. 'Please—call me Michael.'

Melanie nodded. 'Did Jamal have any girlfriends here at work?'

'Yes,…she was friendly with Gemma, one of our agents here.'

Melanie asked:

'Is it possible to speak to her?'

Mr Adisa replied:

'If she's in, yes, I don't see why not. Give me a moment please,' he said, and walked out of room.

Melanie sipped her coffee in silence. *Oh that tastes so good! ...So at least we know who she is. Now we need to find out why she was killed and who killed her. Should be simple,* she thought sarcastically; knowing it was probably going to be *anything* but simple!

Moments later the big African leaned around the door and said:

'You're in luck Miss Underwood—follow me.'

Melanie placed her coffee on the side table and followed Mr Adisa through some double doors into a large, open-plan office where some ten or more people were busy at their desks typing and talking into head-mounted microphones.

One of the agents was smiling at Melanie as they approached her desk. Melanie estimated she was in her mid-twenties. She was pretty with shoulder-length, fair hair and she wore Dolce and Gabbana designer glasses; her smile was infectious.

This must be her.

'Gemma, this is Melanie Underwood, she's investigating the death of Jamal.'

The young girl stood up and shook hands with Melanie. 'Pleased to meet you,' she said, in a thick Scottish accent, 'are you from the police?'

Melanie shook her head. 'No, I work for a private investigation company called Probe, but we are working for the Metropolitan Police.' Melanie then handed her a calling card.

'How exciting!' Gemma replied.

The tall African interjected: 'If you'll excuse me, I'll leave you two girls to chat for a while.'

Melanie replied:

'Yes, thank you Michael, you've been a great help.'

'Catch you later then,' he said, and walked off.

Gemma invited Melanie to sit on a conference chair next to her desk and whispered:

'Sounds far more interesting than this shitty job!'

'It has its moments,' Melanie replied as the images of the two decapitated heads flashed into her mind.

'Terrible business—I still can't believe she's dead,' the young agent confessed. 'She was such a beautiful girl—and so much in love with *life*.'

'I believe she was your friend, Gemma?'

'Yes, she was.'

'Can you tell me about her?'

Gemma took a deep breath, '…I'll try,' she said, as her eyes began to well up. 'She was a good girl, if you know what I mean? She could have put it about, being so beautiful, but she didn't. She loved expensive things and she loved dressing up. When she came here from Syria she was a Muslim, but that

'Oh yes,' she replied, confidently. 'It seems that this poor woman was doomed from the beginning!'

Chapter 6

UPDATE MEETING NO 1

Probe's Incident Room, 9.00 am, Friday 10 May

'Good morning everyone,' Cornish called out above the chattering of the assembled group and the noise level immediately dropped. 'Please be seated…Thanks for coming to the first of our update meetings. I want to use this time to make sure we are all aware of the latest facts by giving you an opportunity to update us with your various findings… So, let *me* start by updating you with some new information. Forensics have now estimated the time of death to be around eleven o'clock last Sunday evening. As we already know, the bodies were discovered at nine-thirty on Monday morning by the cleaner. There are no fingerprints to go on, no signs of an altercation or a struggle and no sign of forced entry. Forensics have also confirmed that the girl's body had very high levels of the anaesthetic, thiopental, in her blood. I just hope for her sake

43

she was unconscious when she was decapitated… As you know, Mikhailov's cause of death was not decapitation, but a .45 bullet that blew his brains out.'

Tom Weiss commented:

'Our murderer was taking no chances, was he?'

Cornish nodded. 'Without doubt this was in many ways a professional killing, guys…but it's also perplexing.… We have two people killed, but in very different ways, why is that? We need to find the answers.'

'Possibly two different killers?' Melanie suggested.

'You mean by coincidence or planned?'

'I suggest it's more likely to be coincidence. A professional, lone killer wouldn't want to complicate things…Maybe he, or she, only planned to kill the Russian and not his girlfriend; so he drugged the girl and then shot the Russian.'

'What, and someone else killed the girl?'

'I think that's possible,' Melanie stated. 'An honour killing perhaps, because she'd relinquished her faith!'

Cornish looked dubious. 'But one hell of a coincidence, I would suggest.'

'Maybe,' reasoned Melanie.

Cornish continued, 'Okay—let's consider all of the options at this point in time…Zeezee, can you please update us on what you've found out about the Russian?'

Zeezee stood up and walked over to face the gathering. 'Maksim Mikhailov was born in Moscow. He is the twenty-four-year-old son of General Alexandra Ivan Mikhailov, a high-ranking Russian military man, who's recently *disowned* his son and accused him of *spying* for the West! We have no proof that he was actually spying, but it appears that the Russians know something that we don't. Putin tends to come down hard on dissidents, as we've experienced in our own backyard. Within the last three months Mikhailov was granted political asylum here in the UK. But, it must be said, according to GCHQ he has not been politically active during his time here. He has, however, been a highly successful artist over the last few years, selling most of his works to buyers in the Middle East. Incidentally, none of the buyers over there are traceable and his work is selling for six figure sums! Zac has some interesting information too.' Zeezee smiled and then walked back to his seat.

Cornish smiled. 'Over to you then, Zac.'

Zac stood up and cleared his throat. '…Thanks to Melanie we've traced the girl's mobile account. She doesn't seem to have a bank account in the UK, at least not one in her name. We're currently working through a few years worth of her emails and text messages but we've found nothing unusual at the moment.' Zac then sat down again.

Cornish commented:

'No bank account—that's interesting! Thanks Zac. Melanie can you update us more on the girl, please?'

Melanie walked to the front and faced the team. She paused for a brief moment to collect her thoughts and then began:

'…The dead girl's name is Jamal Karam. She was a twenty-two-year-old refugee from Syria. Both her parents and her three sisters were killed in the war. She escaped with her brother and they both arrived in the UK four years ago. Both of them are illegal immigrants. Her brother's name is Sami, a twenty-year-old devout Muslim, who has disowned his sister since she gave up the Muslim faith after arriving here. He apparently lives somewhere in London, but as yet, we haven't managed to trace him. We have a photo of him, taken with his family, recovered from the apartment,' Melanie held it up, 'but it was probably taken some ten years ago. According to a close friend of hers, the Russian—not surprisingly known to his friends as Max— was the only boyfriend she'd ever had. But please be aware, we have *nothing* to *substantiate* this information about Jamal Karam at the moment, it's only what we've learned from this close friend of hers and her boss at the agency where she worked… That's it so far, guys.'

'Thanks, Melanie, good work…Tom—see what you can find out about her brother.'

'Will do, sir,' Weiss responded. 'I'll take a wander around the East End and have a *chat* with a few people.'

Cornish nodded and replied: 'Good man!'

*

Melanie topped up Cornish's wine glass. 'I sense that something's bothering you about this case, Alan.'

Cornish smiled and sipped his wine. 'Not much gets past you does it, my love?'

Melanie smirked. '...What is it, Alan, what's bothering you?'

'...I'm not sure, love. But you're right, *something's* bothering me... The river's very tranquil tonight,' he said, leaning on the balcony of the roof-garden.

'Unlike your restless *mind!*' Melanie responded.

'Do you think we're being used as a scapegoat?'

Melanie thought about the question for a while... 'To what end?' she asked.

'I think there are things about this case that we haven't been told.'

'What do you mean?'

Cornish turned to face Melanie. 'I'm not sure yet, but I intend to find out.'

Melanie moved close to Cornish and kissed him on the lips. 'I'm sure you'll work it out, darling,' she said.

'Maybe—but I think I'm going to need your help.'

Melanie stroked his face with her fingertips. 'You've got it, you know that,' she replied. '…Come on, let's go downstairs, the fish pie will be ready.'

'Good idea, I'm starving. Have you checked the mail today, love?' Cornish asked.

'No, I haven't.'

'I'll check it whilst you serve up,' he said, sitting down at the dining table and sifting through the mail. 'There's one here addressed to you in hand-written ink,' he said, 'you don't see that very often, do you?' Cornish handed the letter to Melanie.

'Who could that be from? Anyway—let's eat first, love.'

As they ate their evening meal Melanie kept glancing at the letter.

Cornish noticed. 'Open it if you want to.'

'I'm intrigued,' she said, quickly opening the envelope with a table knife.

Cornish watched as she unfolded a number of small handwritten pages. When she scanned the last page, Melanie raised her hand to her mouth in shock.

'What's the matter?' Cornish asked.

'It's from Vera Parsons!' she said.

'What!' Cornish exclaimed in astonishment.

Ten days ago they'd both attended her funeral. A quiet affair at a local crematorium in Cambridge after Vera had died peacefully in her sleep at the Grange Nursing Home.

Apparently, it had been Vera's wish not to have her funeral in a church. Her service was attended by just a handful of people. Some from the Grange who just wanted a day out and Carol the carer, there to look after them, and a few strangers Melanie didn't recognise, who probably "*just liked a good funeral.*"

Listening to the lady standing on the podium giving the eulogy, it was evident, very quickly, that little of the detail of Vera's life was known to her. In fact Melanie doubted if she'd ever met Vera at all. Melanie probably knew more about Vera's extraordinary life than anyone else and she was tempted to interject on more than one occasion during the impersonal, Catholic like, lacklustre speech—but she resisted. Images of Vera sitting on the garden bench enjoying a cigarette and reminiscing about her early years; years when she was clearly very happy and in love with life flooded into Melanie's mind and she allowed herself a wry smile when she thought about Porky and Vera's all empowering cookie jar. It was then that she realised that *most* things she knew about Vera were probably best left unsaid.

Chapter 7

THE LETTER

'What does it say?' Cornish asked, excitedly.

Melanie wiped tears from her eyes as she read the pages. 'Listen to this,' she said, and then dictated the following letter:

Dearest Melanie

When you read this letter I will be gone from this world; a world which, I must confess, brought me little pleasure during my lifetime. But thankfully I was lucky enough to experience love; the love my father showed me, before he was tragically killed. After his death I was subjected to the worst kind of depravity, the kind that scars someone and distorts their view of life forever.

Thankfully, there were wonderful moments that brought me pleasure and great joy and one of those moments was when you, Melanie, walked into my life. I can't deny my initial feelings of jealousy towards you. Your beauty reminded me so much of my younger self and made me aware of what time had cruelly taken from me; my joie de vivre. But, as if by magic, your presence somehow helped to invigorate my old and tired bones.

Regrettably for me my life has played out very differently to yours and I do so hope from the bottom of my heart that you and your handsome man spend the rest of your lives together; loving and caring for each other, every moment of every single day.

Please accept my sincere apologies for the lies that I proliferated with such ease, and, if I'm honest, with unashamed enjoyment too. You must understand that I was an old lady with nothing left in my life to look forward to.

51

Your company and the hours we spent together were my salvation.

I'm sure, as a young psychologist, you'll be interested to know that over the years I taught myself to believe in what I wanted to believe; simply because the real truth was far too painful to bear.

I want you to understand that I'm not proud of what I did, but I don't regret killing any of those evil people; except perhaps for one, a young thief in a London market when I was just a young girl—he didn't deserve to die. The others deserved everything they got, including Tony. How cruel and ironic was that? The only man I ever loved and he turned out to be the Devil incarnate.

But you must understand, I had no choice, I had to kill him too.

Please don't judge me. If there is a God, then He will be my judge.

Yours in eternal gratitude

Vera

Cornish looked at Melanie in stunned silence. Finally, he said:

'Well, now we know for certain who killed the doctor.'

'She really took me for a ride, didn't she? *That* was a lesson in how to *manipulate* the mind of a psychologist—for Christ's sake!'

'And a lesson you'll *never* forget… But if it's any consolation, she took us all for a ride… Vera Parsons—the serial killer who was never caught.'

Melanie sighed. 'I'm glad she didn't go to the gallows; she had a terrible start in life, and yet she still maintained her own set of twisted morals. I admire her for that.'

Cornish nodded and said:

'It's just a shame that she decided to be judge, jury and *executioner!'*

Chapter 8

BY MEANS OF OTHERS

The previous March

Sami Karam arrived at the East London mosque and parked his scooter outside the main entrance. The front doors were open and people were arriving for the evening speech by a young man that some were accusing of being a radical fundamentalist. A number of the members had argued that he should not be allowed access to the mosque, but, it was eventually decided by the Imam to invite him to give a talk, on the proviso that his speech would not encourage religious extremism, or stir up any kind of racial hatred.

The young Muslim was excited to hear what this apparently contentious visitor would have to say and so he made his way into the mosque, full of anticipation and intrigue. But first, it was time for prayers, time to read the Quran; time to read

God's own instructions and to understand what was required from man, before he departs this world.

Later that evening, some of the answers—explained to him on the bus ride home by the *mysterious* tall and bearded visitor with the dark, piercing eyes—he really wasn't expecting. Tonight was no time for sleeping—tonight he would sit in his tiny bedsit and read from the Quran; God's instructions suddenly had a *new* meaning!

In the name of God, the Most Gracious, the Most Merciful

He read from: (Al-Hajj) The Pilgrimage 22:38

God will surely defend the believers. God does not love the perfidious and the ungrateful. Permission to fight is granted to those who are attacked, because they have been wronged—God indeed has the power to help them—they are those who have been driven out of their homes unjustly, only because they said, 'Our Lord is God.' If God did not repel the aggression of some people by means of others, cloisters and churches and synagogues and mosques, wherein the name of God is much invoked, would surely be destroyed. God will surely help him who helps His cause—God is indeed powerful and mighty.

The *tantalising* suggestion of him going to Afghanistan to become a *jihadi* bewitched him so much that his whole body trembled with excitement. He repeated the words he had just read from the Quran:

'Permission to fight is granted to those who are attacked—if God did not repel the aggression of some people by means of others, cloisters and churches and synagogues and mosques, wherein the name of God is much invoked, would surely be destroyed... By means of others,' he said, 'by means of *others*.' The bedside lamp illuminated his wide-eyed expression—God's words illuminated his mind.

*

Tom Weiss was gradually becoming comfortable with the streets of the East End. It was a place that many people from rural areas of Britain would find bewildering. The majority of people living there were immigrants and the shops and supermarkets reflected their wide gastronomic tastes; the air was thick with the smell of exotic, eastern spices and scents and their vivid colours easily competed with the bright, street-art graffiti that daubed the walls and buildings. The metropolis was bustling with cosmopolitan shoppers and sightseers and the plethora of smells and colours reminded Tom Weiss of the street markets of Manhattan Island; the place he chose to leave behind, to find a new life and hopefully rid his mind of the demons that tormented him.

Most people in the East End had no problem with an American walking the streets and Weiss always treated everyone with respect. But there were some individuals who hated *anything* to do with America and Weiss knew that; he also knew who *most* of his enemies were.

With the sun setting and just a photograph of a very young Sami Karam in his pocket, Weiss set about doing what he was good at; finding people.

It was going to be a long night walking around London, so some hot street-food was definitely a priority. Tonight he fancied stir-fried noodles with chicken and prawns, tossed in a flaming wok; and he knew exactly where to get it.

Chapter 9

A SIBERIAN ICEBOX

Four years before Maksim Mikhailov's death, at General Alexandra Mikhailov's private living-quarters (at a military location in central Siberia)

'I hate this place!... Why do I have to spend any more of my fucking time in depressing *iceboxes* like these?' Maksim Mikhailov asked. 'They're just like prisons. There's no sunlight, no trees, no birds, no fresh air to breath; it's hell for me to live below ground, Father... I detest it and you know that. So why do you *insist* on me visiting? There is nothing here for me, now that Mother has gone. It just makes me so unhappy. I can take care of myself now, I'm not a child anymore—I'm twenty years of age, Father!'

General Mikhailov stopped eating and raised his cold, piercing eyes to look down the long table at his son. '…These places are *necessary*,' he said, sternly, 'and I made a promise to your mother that I would take care of you; something you *obviously* do not appreciate.'

'I appreciate my expensive education—but,' Maksim raised his hands, despondently, 'I don't appreciate coming here anymore. Why are these places so *necessary* anyway?'

'…Because our *great* country is under constant threat from our enemies. They *hate* us because we are superior to them. They *envy* our way of life and they spy on us with their satellites, twenty-four-hours-a-day. But, these *underground* military bases, which *you* have had the *privilege* of visiting— are safe from their prying eyes. These places are where we develop our military superiority and, our military superiority will be our saviour one day. We are building more and more weaponry every day and the West has no concept of our military might, because their satellites don't work down here!' The General smiled, smugly, but quickly frowned before continuing: 'If you were a real man—a *soldier*—like me,' he stressed, 'you would understand these things, but you're not a *real* man are you, Maksim? You're a pitiful excuse for a man. Someone who wants to waste his life—*painting!*'

The young Mikhailov considered his father's words for a moment and then replied:

'But just imagine, Father, if we were all painters, there would be no need for armies, or weapons, and talk of enemies, and there would be no need to *fear* our neighbours... What would you do in a world at peace, Father? Would you be a mechanic or a baker maybe, or would you rather slaughter pigs all day so your hands could be covered in blood? Would that make you happy?'

The General's face turned red and he began to tremble with anger. '*Real men,*' he yelled, '*real men* are born to be soldiers, and real men are prepared to die defending their country. Real men do not *paint!*'

The young Russian sighed. '...I'm a terrible disappointment to you, aren't I?'

The General replied, tersely; his chest heaving with rage:

'...I cannot deny it... I cannot *believe* you are my son! I carry my shame with a heart as heavy as lead.'

The young Russian smiled at his father. 'Well, I'm sorry if I'm a disappointment to you, but I am what I am.'

With a condescending sneer, the General asked:

'And what exactly are you?'

'I'm an artist, Father—I paint; it's in my blood.'

The General stood up and threw his napkin on the table, spilling his glass of wine. 'Then it's your mother's fucking blood that flows through your veins—not mine!... Tomorrow I will arrange for you to be flown back to Moscow.' 'I never want to see you again—under any circumstances—is that clear?' he said, and not waiting for a reply, the General stormed out of the room, leaving his evening meal unfinished.

Maksim Mikhailov sat in pensive silence for a few moments listening to the attenuating sound of his father's footsteps and watching the red wine drip from the table, like spilled blood, onto the floor. *What a sad, delusional man—I hate you—I've always hated you,* he thought; and then he burst out laughing.

Eventually, regaining his composure, he said, quietly:

'The *only* people who know the secret *underground* military locations are the Russian military—oh yes—and *me*—a pitiful excuse for a man.'

The young man got up from the dining table and walked over to a framed photograph of his late mother. He picked up the frame and stroked her image tenderly. 'I miss you so much,' he said, 'you understand why I have to do this, don't you, Mother? I *know* you do... Thankfully, I have *your* blood flowing through my veins.'

Chapter 10

SOMEBODY WANTED HIM DEAD

'What's the latest, Zeezee?' Cornish asked.

Zeezee spun around on his desk chair and faced Cornish. 'It appears that our man Max, escaped from Russia on a false passport three years ago. He made his way across Europe, through Germany and France, before using his real passport to get into the UK. He then claimed political asylum here on the grounds that he would be killed if he was returned to Russia.'

'Because the Russians thought he was a spy?' Cornish asked.

'He claimed to be a dissident, although there's no real evidence to suggest that, other than his paintings of course; and they were done in the UK.'

Cornish nodded. 'Well, *somebody* wanted him dead, which surely means he was either a threat to Putin's regime—because he *knew* something of real value to the West—or he had something of real value for *sale*. And let's not forget, his father did accuse him of spying.'

Zeezee stroked his beard. '…MI6 are adamant that he wasn't working for them and Interpol have confirmed that he was not on their radar. By the way, forensics say the bullet that killed him was probably a .45 GAP fired from close range. The killer took the casing with him.'

'That's what assassins do, they leave no trace behind them. The bullet was probably fired from a Glock.'

'Yeah, most likely,' Zeezee agreed.

Cornish walked back to his office, tapping his fingertips together, deep in thought.

Chapter 11

CHAMPAGNE AND ROYAL OSCIETRA CAVIAR

Ministry of Sound, London—three years ago.

Jamal Karam knew exactly how to get what she wanted and most of the things she wanted were expensive. Men wanted *her* because she was breathtakingly beautiful, elegant and enigmatic. With her flawless, dark, olive complexion, shoulder length, raven-black hair and dark, sultry eyes she could have been a top London hostess, earning thousands of pounds a week. She played her men like an expert angler played a prize fish; reeling them in, then letting them run until they were near exhaustion, and then reeling them in again, but never quite landing them; always letting them off the hook to play them another day. Some of her jealous admirers called her a prick-teaser and gold-digger; some suggested she was actually a lesbian—but *nobody* ever called her a spy.

It was Maksim Mikhailov's first visit to the Ministry of Sound. He was celebrating the sale of his first painting. He had money in his pocket, seats in the VIP area, champagne and pre-ordered Royal Oscietra caviar from Russia on the table. All he needed now was a beautiful woman to keep him company.

It wasn't long before he saw her, looking at him, smiling; and it wasn't long before he'd invited her to join him for a glass of champagne.

'My name is Maksim, I'm an artist,' he said.

'Pleased to meet you, Maksim. My name is Jamal,' she replied as they shook hands.

'Please,' the Russian said, offering Jamal a glass of champagne.

'You're very kind,' she said, taking the drink and sitting down next to her host. 'So what kind of an artist are you, Maksim?'

The Russian smiled, remembering the exhilaration he'd felt earlier in the day when he'd sold his first work. 'I paint with oils.'

'Is that your job?' Jamal asked

'Yes, it's how I make my living.'

'You have an accent.'

'Yes,—I'm from Russia, but I live here now. How about you?'

'I'm from Syria, but I also live here now.'

Mikhailov looked into her eyes, wanting to know more about this spellbindingly beautiful creature who'd just walked into his life.

Jamal, however, already knew a lot about the man with the ice-blue eyes, long, wavy, blonde hair and the diamond stud in his ear.

'So why did you leave Russia?' she asked after sipping her champagne.

Mikhailov laughed. 'Because I *hated* it! Russia is for warriors not artists,' he said.

Jamal laughed. 'That's a good reason I suppose,' she said.

'And you left Syria because of the war, right?'

'Right! And now I've *sampled* freedom I cannot live the lifestyle of a Muslim woman any longer; a lifestyle where we cannot eat at the same table as our men! I want my freedom, I want to enjoy my life and feel equal to anyone and everyone.'

Mikhailov listened in enthralled silence, transfixed by Jamal Karam's radiant beauty and confidence. 'It would be a shame to cover such a beautiful face,' he said.

Jamal smiled coyly. '…So what was it that you hated about Russia?' she asked.

'…I hated *everything* about Russia—except for the caviar,' he said, as he topped up Jamal's glass. Mikhailov waved to a waitress and ordered another bottle of champagne. '…My father is a Russian General—old school. I swear he had his heart cut out the day he was born.'

Jamal giggled and moved a little closer to Mikhailov.

The Russian looked into her eyes and said:

'I am a massive disappointment to my father.'

'Why is that?'

'Because I didn't want to be a soldier prepared to die for my country. Russia is arming itself, convinced that an attack from the West is imminent. They have numerous, secret, underground facilities,' Mikhailov shrugged, 'bomb factories— all over Russia, overseen by *my* father, and believe me, my father would love nothing better than another war; he *thrives* on aggression and suspicion. He is such a sad, misguided man. But I have only ever wanted to be an artist and he could not accept that. Artists—he often reminded me—were *scum*, superfluous to the greater cause.'

'…What about your mother?' Jamal asked.

'Sadly, my mother died a few years ago.'

'Oh…I'm sorry,' she said, and rested her hand on his. Their eyes met and they slowly moved closer to each other. Tentatively, their lips touched and he could feel her sweet, pulsing breath on his face. The Ministry of Sound's pumping beat and kaleidoscope of colours faded into the distance.

Jamal pulled back and smiled, confidently.

Mikhailov took a deep breath and exhaled slowly; the pumping beat returned to his ears. He smiled back and gestured to the table:

'…Please… help yourself to some caviar. There is nothing as good as *Russian* Beluga caviar,' he said, confidently, 'and this is the best of them.'

Jamal showed no interest in the caviar. '… So will you return to Russia one day?' she enquired.

'Not possible I'm afraid. They think I'm a spy. If I went back I'd most likely be shot or spend the rest of my days rotting in a Siberian prison.'

'So why do they think you're a spy?' Jamal asked.

'Good question, because I'm not a spy—I'm just an *artist*—with something to sell.'

Jamal frowned. 'Something to sell?' she repeated.

'Yeah—something worth a *lot* of money!'

'You mean your paintings?'

Mikhailov laughed and sipped his champagne smugly. 'Something *far* more valuable than that!'

Jamal moved closer again. 'Like what?'

The Russian's eyes glanced all around and then he answered quietly:

'Top-secret military information. The only problem is—I don't know who to sell it to—I just know it's worth a *lot* of money.'

For a while, Jamal seemed focused on some distant object; then a barely perceptible smile passed over her lips and she said:

'I have a lot of contacts and I know a lot of very influential people… I just *might* be able to help you—if you're interested?'

Mikhailov immediately sat up straight. 'Really?'

Jamal nodded.

'So what exactly is it that *you* do?' he asked, intrigued by the beautiful but mysterious woman's offer.

'I find people for a very exclusive headhunting company in town and I meet a lot of *extremely* rich people; some of them I meet through work and the others are simply—admirers—who mistakenly believe that money can buy them *any* woman they want; but, let me assure you, *my* body is not for sale.'

'…Well, in that case I would like to make a toast,' he said, holding up his glass. 'To you, virtuous lady, and our new business venture.'

Jamal chuckled and chinked glasses. 'To us,' she said and returned the smile, relaxed in the knowledge that her evening was going *exactly* to plan.

Chapter 12

MELANIE'S INTROSPECTION

Cornish walked over to Melanie and put his arms around her. 'Are you going to tell me what's bothering you?'

'I'm okay.'

Cornish raised his eyebrows in question.

'I need a glass of wine,' she said.

'Red or white?'

'…I fancy some red tonight,' she said.

Cornish poured out two glasses of red and handed Melanie a glass. 'That sauce tastes good, love, he said, after dipping a spoon into the saucepan.'

Melanie smiled. 'Ten minutes,' she said, and sipped her wine before kissing Cornish.

'Are you going to tell me, then?' he asked.

'It's nothing love—honestly.'

'If you don't tell me, I'll drink the rest of the wine.'

Melanie smiled and sighed. It's just…'

'It's just what?'

'…I'm worried that you might think I'm not doing my job properly.'

Cornish frowned. 'Whatever gave you that idea?'

Melanie took a long gulp of wine. '...Well—*firstly* I'm supposed to be a psychologist and Vera Parsons wrapped me around her little finger and *manipulated* me like I was a puppet on a string. I was taken in, hook, line and sinker.'

Cornish went to say something but Melanie raised her finger.

'*Secondly,* I'm sick all over a policeman's boots when I visit a crime scene... It's not sounding too *professional* is it?'

Cornish topped up their wine glasses and said:

'During my career in the police, do you think that I made any mistakes?'

Melanie managed a weak smile.

'... It just means that you're human and you have feelings and that's nothing to be ashamed of. We *all* make mistakes Melanie, but the trick is to *learn* from them and never make the *same* mistake *twice*. That way you develop as an individual and become, over a period of time, a true professional. The next Vera you meet, and you will meet one, you'll treat very differently. You'll *question* her differently and you'll stay focussed on what *you* need to know, and not what *she* wants you to know. But, as I said to you before, Vera was a special case—she was clever and calculating—she was a serial killer who was never caught and if it's any consolation to you, she took me in, too; hook, line and sinker.'

Melanie wrapped her arms around Cornish and kissed him again. 'Thank you,' she said.

'My pleasure. How's the spaghetti doing?'

'Drain it off please, we're ready to eat.'

During their evening meal, Cornish and Melanie talked about the London murders and what seemed to be an impossible case to solve with such a minimum amount of evidence to go on.

Melanie said:

'I find Jamal Karam rather intriguing. She was obviously a bit of a rebel; someone who craved life's luxuries—someone, according to her work colleague, who was about to become very rich, very soon.'

'Wishful thinking maybe? Marrying a successful artist?'

'Maybe… I can't explain it—it's just a gut feeling at the moment.'

Cornish smiled. 'Always trust your instincts.'

'Yes,—I intend to,' Melanie replied and sipped her wine. Her confidence was beginning to returning. 'I love you, Alan Cornish,' she said. 'How do you fancy an early night?'

Cornish smiled. 'You strike a hard bargain,' he replied.

Their relationship had grown stronger over the last year and Cornish was spending more and more time at Melanie's place by the river; it just seemed natural to the both of them. Cornish's little, terraced house in Trumpington was now hardly used and the back garden was looking very neglected; the lawn needed cutting and the flower beds needed weeding. Before he'd met Melanie the little, two-bedroomed place served its purpose, but now, he just wanted to be with her at her place; sitting snuggled up together on the sofa around the open fire on the dark, winter nights, and up on the roof-garden on balmy, summer nights, eating and drinking wine and laughing about the poor policeman's boots!

Cornish knew he'd found the woman he wanted to spend the rest of his life with and, thankfully, he had no idea what the future had planned for them!

Chapter 13

THE YOUNG JIHADI

Probe's Offices, Cambridge

Melanie walked into the interview room not really knowing what to expect. Maksim Mikhailov's cleaning lady was there, dressed all-in-black and wearing a hijab, she was sitting at the table looking extremely nervous. Sitting next to her was a young, lady interpreter by the name of Sofie. Melanie smiled at the cleaning lady but got no response as she settled on a chair at the table directly opposite her.

'Good afternoon, my name is Melanie Underwood and I'm investigating the murders of Maksim Mikhailov and Jamal Karam.'

The middle-aged Arab woman looked at the interpreter with an expression of bewilderment as the interpreter explained to her what Melanie had just said. Speaking in Arabic the woman replied, tearfully.

The interpreter looked at Melanie and said:

'She says that she's innocent. It is against her beliefs to kill another person.'

Melanie smiled. *If only everyone thought that way.* 'Please tell her not to worry, but as part of our enquiries it is necessary for me to ask her a few questions, and to confirm, we offered Miss Halabi the right to have a solicitor present but she declined. Is that correct?'

The interpreter nodded in agreement.

'Can you answer yes or no for the record,' Melanie asked.

'Yes,—that's correct,' replied the interpreter.

During the interview the Arab woman confirmed to Melanie that when she arrived at the apartment at 09.30 on Monday morning and opened the front door, she saw Jamal Karam's decapitated body tied to the chair. She said that she ran to the bathroom to be sick, only to find the Russian decapitated in the bath. She stressed that she must have fainted because the next thing she remembered was lying on the floor looking at her phone and it was 09.55. It was then that she ran out of the apartment in a panic and into the street. She collapsed on the pavement and someone called for an ambulance. It was after that incident that the police discovered the bodies in the apartment.

Melanie checked her watch. The interview had lasted twenty-eight minutes and Melanie was sure that there was nothing more to learn from the cleaner. Melanie said for the record:

'The time now is two-twenty-seven and the interview with Miss Halabi is concluded.' Melanie then switched off the recorder.—'I'm all done here, please thank Miss Halabi for her cooperation. She's free to go, but for the moment she must not leave the country under any circumstances,' Melanie stressed to the interpreter.

The interpreter spoke to the cleaner and for the first time the Arab woman smiled at Melanie. Melanie smiled back and they shook hands.

I've just told an illegal immigrant that she's not allowed to leave the country—no wonder she's bloody smiling!

Twenty minutes later Melanie was sitting in Cornish's office discussing the interview.

'It wasn't of much help really; nothing more than what we knew from her statement.'

'She doesn't look like the type that would decapitate two people, does she?' Cornish suggested.

'No—not at all; she looks quite frail.'

'Any news on Jamal Karam?'

'Not a thing. She's a bit of an enigma that woman.'

'What about her brother?' Cornish asked.

'Nothing. Tom has been looking for him for nearly a week now and if Tom can't find someone, then they don't exist.'

Just then the phone rang and Cornish picked up the handset. 'Cornish here,' he said, and for a while he listened in silence. Then he responded:

'Tom, I'm putting you on speaker—I've got Melanie here.'

'Hi Tom,' Melanie called out.

'Hi Melanie,' he replied.

'Tom, for Melanie's benefit, can you start from the beginning again please?'

'Sure can.—I've found the Mosque where Sami Karam attended and asked the locals a few questions. He apparently went to Afghanistan to become a jihadi and hasn't been seen since.'

'When did he leave the country, Tom?' Melanie asked.

'March of this year, apparently on a flight to Turkey. Zeezee checked with Customs and he re-entered the country, via Heathrow, ten days before the murders took place. But there's no sign of him on his old patch.'

Cornish looked at Melanie and said: 'He's gone to ground.'

'Thanks Tom; don't give up on him and keep up the good work.'

'Yes, sir,' came the reply.

Cornish ended the call and immediately started to tap his fingertips together.

'…What's bothering you?' Melanie asked.

'…The bullet in his head,' he replied. 'I can't see the reason for it, if you're going to cut someone's head off, why shoot them first?'

'Yeah, it doesn't make sense does it?'

Cornish sighed. 'Something's not right with all of this, and at the moment, my love—I can't even *guess* at the answer.'

'We need to find her brother, Alan.'

'Yes, you're right, we do. Let's just hope Tom gets *lucky.*'

Melanie walked behind Cornish and gently massaged his shoulders. 'We could certainly do with some luck,' she said, pensively.

Chapter 14

A VISITOR TO THE UK

Eight days before the London murders

Tomas Soukal watched as the English coastline and the port of Dover loomed closer through the swirling, morning mist. He glanced up at the seagulls that lingered effortlessly overhead, as if they were escorting the ferry to its berth; but the tranquility was broken when a tannoy announcement informed the passengers that they would be docking at Dover shortly and that it was time to go down to the car decks; back to his Mercedes, harbouring the Glock 22.40 pistol and silencer and the dart gun, hidden in the secret boot compartment. Getting guns into the UK was easier this way and when he was done, he could simply dump them—wiped clean.

The assassin took one last drag of his cigarette before flicking it over the handrail into the frothing waves and then he made his way back into the aromatic warmth of the coffee lounge and then down the stairs to the car decks.

Forty minutes later he'd been waved through customs and was heading for London on the M20; the name on his passport was Lucas Janssens—a young man from Antwerp in Belgium. He selected the comfort driving mode on the Merc's centre console and then settled back into the leather driving seat to enjoy a gentle and slow back massage on the journey to the park-and-ride at Croydon; luxury was now something he embraced with open arms. Memories of his childhood street-life, his constant hunger pains, the cold, biting, winter winds and the long, dark nights were now distant, fading memories. He smiled when he thought about being in London again, in an expensive hotel, sleeping on crisp, white Egyptian cotton sheets and enjoying the good food and wine. But he knew that all too soon he would be back on the ferry to Calais and changing the registration plates before the long drive home to Prague—via Germany, of course, for a few day's of relaxation and a visit to his favourite S&M club in Frankfurt; expensive luxuries, all paid for by a bullet to the head of a young Russian. The job would earn him a great deal of money; more money than his drunken father could ever have imagined. It was his way— quick and quiet; nobody could survive a bullet into the forehead from close range. Done quickly, the victim wouldn't have time to react, or even realise what was about to happen. He rehearsed, over and over again in his mind, the two options that he would most likely face—until something distracted him and he stole a glance into the rearview mirror; a police car with blue, flashing lights was approaching fast in the outside lane. He checked his speed—130 kilometres per hour—and immediately slowed down—as his heartbeat quickened. The flashing lights were upon him and the siren started to wail, but the BMW accelerated past him at high speed... He breathed a sigh of relief.

It wasn't him, or his Glock, they were looking for—at least not yet.

Chapter 15

BUT WHY TEN PAINTINGS?

Early April

Maksim Mikhailov watched as an animated Jamal Karam pranced around the apartment, occasionally slowing to sip champagne from the flute delicately balanced between her fingers.

'I tell you Max,' Jamal enthused, 'he was eating out of my hands at the end and the thought of having the *Americans* eating out of *his* hands made him salivate.'

Mikhailov smiled and lit a cigarette. 'Like Pavlov's dogs!'

'Whose dogs?'

The Russian laughed as the young woman waltzed effortlessly around the room, high on success. 'We will sell them the information,' she continued, '*hidden* in ten of your oil paintings. That way no one will suspect us of *anything* and we will be thirty-million-dollars the richer—and *you* will be a very successful artist, my love.'

'And just how do we do that?'

Jamal frowned '...I don't know yet, but I'll think of something,' she said, and continued to prance around the room, deep in thought. '...We'll hide a USB stick in each of the painting's frames...that's what we'll do!' she exclaimed, excitedly refilling her glass, 'we'll drip feed them the information.'

'But why ten paintings?'

'Why not? It means you sell *more* paintings? It'll be good for your reputation as an exciting, new artist that everyone wants to be seen with.'

'To be honest, I really don't care how we do it—just as long as nobody tells President Putin—because there are no pockets in a shroud!'

'Don't worry about a thing—just leave *everything* to me, my love.'

'Everything except the ten paintings!'

'Yes, of course, but that's *your* department, darling. My job is to make us very, very rich. We'll release the paintings one-by-one, every week for ten weeks, as long as they pay us three million dollars on receipt of each one of them. I'll arrange for a joint bank account to be set up outside of the UK. Believe me, I have lot's of streetwise contacts to advise me on the best way to avoid paying tax.'

Mikhailov smiled. 'And what *exactly* am I going to paint?'

'It doesn't matter!'

'It does matter—I'm an artist—it matters to me!'

'Okay, but I'm sure you'll think of something,' Jamal said, slightly irritated by his attitude, 'after all, they're not really interested in the *paintings* are they?'

Mikhailov wasn't listening now. 'I need a theme to work with, if I'm going to paint ten oils,' he said out loud.

'For thirty-million dollars—I'm sure you'll come up with something, Max!'

Mikhailov sank back on the sofa. 'So what am I going to do with fifteen-million dollars?'

Jamal laughed out loud. '…You can do w*hatever* you want, my love,' she replied and quickly downed the remains of her champagne.

'I will have a new studio in the south of France with a balcony overlooking the sea, where I can stand and paint in glorious sunshine. And there I will create masterpieces that will stun the art world and *everyone* will know my name. People will say: "Look—that's a Mikhailov"—just like they recognise a Picasso or a Van Gogh.'

'And I will have glistening diamonds on my fingers and in my ears and I'll drive a Bentley convertible with white leather seats,' Jamal added, as she straddled Mikhailov on the sofa. 'Very soon we will be rich,—rich beyond our *wildest* dreams, my darling, but I need to get that precious information out of that head of yours,' Jamal said, running her fingers through the Russian's hair, ' because it's of no value to us if we can't sell it, is it?'

Mikhailov seemed suddenly inspired. 'Tomorrow, I will start the first of the ten paintings,' he said, excitedly. 'Ideas are already flooding into my imagination. But first I'm going to fuck you.'

Jamal giggled.'I knew you would, my love,' she said.

Chapter 16

WHERE HAVE YOU BEEN?

Sami Karam's whole body trembled with fear. He checked his watch as he walked tentatively towards the mosque that he once frequented—it was five minutes to eight. As the rain fell gently onto the wet street he watched as the main door of the mosque opened and the familiar diminutive figure of the Imam appeared. Karam's pace quickened as he followed the old man across Whitechapel Road. As the Imam entered Greatorex Street, Sami Karam called out his name. The old man stopped, turned and smiled with delight when he finally recognised his young pupil.

'Sami! Where have you been? We have missed you.'

Karam's young face was wracked with fear; raindrops dripped from his hoody. '…Imam, I am in trouble—terrible trouble,' he said, as if he was in pain.

The Imam looked shocked by the young Muslim's dishevelled appearance and fearful words. 'What have you done that is so bad, young man?'

Sami Karam lowered his head in shame. 'I have failed him.'

The Imam shook his head. 'Who have you failed?'

'…I have failed Allah and now I am really scared.'

'I don't understand, young man, how have you failed—?'

It was then that the young Muslim noticed him, standing on the corner of the road. 'I have to go Imam—please pray for my forgiveness,' he said, with urgency and scurried quickly down the road.

The Imam looked back towards the busy Whitechapel Road, at the man standing on the corner and immediately recognised him. 'Oh God,' he murmured, 'what have I done?'

*

'The kid was seen near the mosque last night,' Tom Weiss enthused as he entered Alan Cornish's office. 'It seems like he's on the run and very frightened.'

'How do you know?' Cornish asked, looking up from his desk.

'One of my contacts said that the Imam talked to him near the mosque, just after eight o'clock last night. He said that the kid was scared because he'd *failed* Allah!'

'Failed Allah?'

'That's what he said.'

'We need to find him Tom, and quickly.'

'I know, but it won't be easy, Boss.'

'He's obviously staying around the patch that he's familiar with.' Cornish tapped his fingertips together. 'Failed Allah,' he repeated, pensively. '...Sometimes, Tom, I'm very glad that I'm an atheist.'

Tom Weiss nodded. 'Yeah, me too,' he replied.

Cornish frowned and continued:

'But you don't *run* from Allah, do you? So who is he running from—and why? Was it *him* who decapitated his own sister and the Russian?'

Weiss smiled. 'If it was him, then how come he's failed Allah? Seems to me like he did a very thorough job!'

Cornish chuckled. '*None* of this makes any sense to me.'

'I'm with you on that one, Boss.'

'We need to talk to that Imam.'

'I think you'd have a better chance than me,—me being American, I mean,' Weiss stressed.

'...Umm, I think this might be a job for Melanie,' Cornish said, picking up the phone.

Chapter 17

THE IMAM

Thanks to Tom Weiss, Melanie was aware of the approximate times that the Imam would leave the mosque; thanks to the rigid times set out for Muslims to pray. She walked slowly down Whitechapel Road towards the mosque, patiently and somewhat anxiously, waiting for the religious man to leave the building. In her pocket she carried a photograph of the man she was hoping to meet. He was, according to Tom Weiss, about five feet one and he walked with a distinctive limp.

It was now late afternoon and judging by the number of people leaving the mosque, Salat al-'asr prayers had just finished. Melanie checked her watch—three thirty-nine. *Just as you predicted, Tom,* Melanie thought. It was another thirty minutes though before the Imam appeared at the front of the mosque wearing a white cap and loosely fitting, light-coloured, cotton suit. Melanie spotted him immediately and covered her head with a scarf before approaching him. She'd taken Tom's advice and was wearing a long, dark, loosely fitting dress.

'Imam,' she said.

The little man glanced at her with an expression of curiosity. 'Yes—can I help you?'

Melanie approached him. 'My name is Melanie Underwood. I'm working for the Metropolitan Police, investigating a recent double murder. Can I please ask you a few questions?'

The Imam looked shocked by Melanie's request. 'I can assure you that I know *nothing* about any murder, young lady.'

Melanie quickly glanced around her and noticed a nearby cafe.

'I need to speak to a young man who I believe you know; I'm hoping he may be able to assist us in our enquiries... Can I buy you a drink? A cup of tea perhaps?'

The Imam forced a thin smile, nodded reluctantly and followed Melanie to the cafe. Inside the cafe they sat at a window table in view of the mosque and Melanie ordered a tea for the Imam and coffee for herself.

'Thank you for your time, Imam,' she said.

'Who is this man you are looking for?' he asked, but Melanie suspected he already knew the answer.

Melanie replied:

'A young man named Sami Karam. His *sister* was one of the two people murdered.'

The Imam lowered his head for a moment then slowly looked up at Melanie. 'I know him,' he said.

'Do you know where I can find him?'

The Imam shook his head.

'We believe he is in hiding. Do you know who he might be hiding from?'

The Imam became agitated by Melanie's question.

'His *life* may be in danger,' Melanie stressed.

'I…I don't think I can help you,' he said, nervously.

A waitress arrived with their drinks and placed them on the table. 'One tea and one coffee,' she said. ' Can I get you anything to eat from the menu?' she asked.

'No, thank you,' Melanie replied, somewhat impatiently.

Once the waitress had gone Melanie asked:

'Do you know where he is, Imam?'

'No,—I'm sorry—I don't.'

'Do you know *why* he is hiding?'

The Imam fidgeted, nervously before shaking his head. 'No, he replied.'

You're lying, thought Melanie.

Then suddenly the Imam produced a small notepad and pen from his pocket and scribbled something on it. He tore off the page and folded it in half. 'Maybe this will help you,' he said. 'I'm sorry but I have to go now. I'm sorry that I didn't tell you anything.' The Imam stood up and walked out of the cafe. For a few moments Melanie just stared at the folded piece of paper on the table, wrestling with the Imam's words: *"I'm sorry that I didn't tell you anything,"* then she opened the note and read the message.

*

The cold, rat-infested, concrete shell that had been Sami Karam's hideaway for more than two-weeks stretched away in front of him as he slouched forlornly on the flattened cardboard boxes that were his makeshift bed. Next to him was the remains of his last meal: an apple core, a banana skin and a half-empty bottle of water.

The guilt he was feeling over his sister's death was beginning to tear him apart. What possessed him to do such a thing? In Syria he'd experienced hunger many times, he'd feared for his life many times too. But the *guilt* was overpowering, consuming him from the inside out, like an aggressive tumour. He was a Jihadi, he'd been trained to kill, killing infidels was *expected* of him because that is what infidels deserved; it was written in the Quran—It was God's words.

What would happen to him on the Day of Judgement? Would he be accepted into Paradise or cast out to Hell for eternity, for what he had done?

The young Muslim slowly lifted his head and glanced over to the rusting, metal stairs that gave access to the five upper floors and rooftop of the derelict warehouse. It was then that the solution to his problems came to him in an instant.

The time had come—it would be quick—before *they* got to him.

Paradise or Hell?

He realised that in the next few minutes he would know his fate.

He stood up and walked towards the stairs, strangely calm and controlled; a feeling of euphoria surged through his body. Would he be welcomed into Paradise by his parents and his sisters?

A spiralling dust cloud billowed into the air as a black Mercedes Benz powered its way towards the warehouse. Inside the vehicle, two hooded men, dressed in black, were armed with meat cleavers and a pistol. It was time to slaughter the very man that they had trained to slaughter infidels.

Chapter 18

PARADISE OR HELL?

'Melanie, listen to me—wait for backup to arrive. Do not go in there alone. This guy is *extremely* dangerous,' Cornish stressed down the phone.

'Yes, okay —I understand.'

'There's an armed response unit *and* the bomb squad on their way to the site. Co-ordinate with them when you get there, okay. I'm leaving Cambridge now by helicopter and I'll be with you as soon as I can. Don't approach him, Melanie. This guy is a *jihadi*. The place may be wired with explosives.'

'Don't worry Alan, I'll be fine,' Melanie replied. 'I've got Tom here with me.'

'That's good,' replied Cornish. 'See you soon—and stay safe, because I love you,' he said, before ending the call.

Cornish knew that this man was probably the *key* to the investigation. He needed him alive. He scooped up his car-keys from his desk and hurried out of the office to get to the local airfield, just five minutes from the office, where, hopefully, the police helicopter and sniper that he'd requested would be waiting to fly him to London.

Having chosen his imminent fate, the young Muslim climbed the metal stairs in a trance-like state until he reached the rooftop.   There was a warm sun shining and a gentle breeze blowing as he walked towards the building's edge.

Below, at ground level, Melanie was horror struck when she saw the young Muslim appear on the rooftop. She watched him as he climbed up onto the parapet of the building, before standing there, motionless, with his eyes closed.

'Oh my God, he's going to jump!' she cried out.

Stealth like, the armed response unit had arrived and was now in place in front of the building. Twelve officers aimed their rifles at him, waiting for the instruction to shoot.

'Don't shoot him,' Melanie called out to the officer in charge, 'he's not armed!'

Inside the building, the two hooded men climbed the metal stairs. One of them was carrying a machete, the other was clenching the Glock handgun that had been used to kill Maksim Mikhailov.

'Do not fire until ordered to do so!' came the response to Melanie's request.

Melanie's mobile rang and she answered it. 'Yes, Alan?'

'I'm five minutes away. What's happening?'

'The warehouse is surrounded with armed police and Sami Karam has just appeared on the roof. I think he's going to jump, Alan.'

'…Is there any way we can stop him, Melanie? …Is it possible to talk him down from up there? …Melanie—we need him alive!'

'Yes, yes, I hear you Alan. I'll do what I can, okay?'

'Yes, okay—I'll be with you soon, my love.'

Melanie slipped the phone into her pocket. 'I need to speak to him,' she called out to the officer in charge. Moments later a megaphone was thrust into her hands.

Melanie walked a few paces forward and lifted the megaphone to her mouth and began to speak:

'Sami Karam, my name is Melanie. There is no need to be afraid. No one here wants to hurt you. Can we talk? Can I come up there to talk to you? I will be on my own, I promise.'

The young Muslim stared down at Melanie; his face racked with fear.

'Sami, will you talk to me?' Melanie insisted as she walked closer to the building. 'I am not armed,' she stressed and laid the megaphone on the floor in front of her. To her amazement, Karam nodded.

Turning around she called out to the commanding officer, 'I'm going up—alone.' Then she turned to Tom Weiss and said:

'I'll be okay Tom, but I need to go alone,' and she walked briskly towards the building. Inside, she quickly noticed the metal stairs and climbed them as fast as she could. Her heart was pounding in her chest as she reached the last flight and there she paused for a moment to catch her breath. Looking up she could see a small square of blue sky. What was she going to say? They wanted him alive—*She* wanted him alive!

Melanie climbed the last few stairs and squinted as she walked out into the bright sunshine. To her right she immediately noticed the young Muslim. To her relief he'd stepped down from the edge of the building.

'Thank you for allowing me to talk to you,' she said, with a smile.

'No!' the young Muslim cried out just before the sound of a gunshot rang out in Melanie's right ear. Sami Karam's head jolted backwards as the bullet hit him and he collapsed on the floor. In an instant the gunman ran forward and picked up the young Muslim. Melanie froze in disbelief as she watched him hurl Karam's limp body off the roof. It was then that she felt a hand grip her forehead like a clamp and the cold steel of a machete blade pressing into her throat. The last thing Melanie was aware of, before she passed out, was the pounding sound of the approaching helicopter's rotor blades.

As the pilot approached the roof of the warehouse, Alan Cornish could see Melanie being restrained by one of the men.

A momentary flash of sunlight glinted off the polished machete blade pressed against her throat. The other man was pointing a hand gun at the helicopter.

Cornish said to the pilot:

'Can we land on the roof?'

The pilot quickly assessed the situation and nodded his approval.

'Okay,' Cornish said, 'land near the far left corner—they don't know we have a sniper on board.'

The pilot guided the chopper onto the roof and landed as instructed. Quickly, Cornish opened his door and climbed out. He crouched down and walked around the front of the chopper before raising his hands in the air to face the two assailants.

Dust and paper swirled into the air. The gunman pointed his gun at Cornish. 'Stop there!'

Cornish halted.

The gunman shouted:

'*That* is our ticket out of here,' he shouted, wielding his gun at the chopper, 'otherwise the girl has her throat ripped out in front of your eyes.'

'Please—let the girl go,' Cornish called out, biding for a few seconds of precious time.

The gunman laughed. 'Let her *go*? Do you think I'm *mad*? She is safe *only* as long as *we* get off this roof alive—so the girl is coming with us.'

Cornish's mind was working overtime as he assessed the situation. He quickly realised Melanie was unconscious by the way her head was slouched and how the man with the machete was struggling to hold up her limp body. Cornish gave a furtive glance into the rear of the helicopter and clenched his right hand. The man holding Melanie immediately recoiled backwards from the force of the marksman's bullet that ripped through his head. As the gunman's mouth opened in disbelief his head exploded as the marksman fired his second shot.

Cornish ran towards Melanie who'd collapsed on top of her assailant. Her neck was bloodied but he could see she was still alive and he gently lifted her head.

'Melanie—Speak to me!' he said, slapping her face gently. 'Melanie! *Melanie!*'

Melanie slowly opened her eyes to see Cornish looking down at her. '… Am I glad to see you,' she said, before turning her head towards the bloodied corpse next to her and promptly fainting again.

'That's my girl!' Cornish said with a broad smile, as he lifted her into his arms.

Behind him there was a sudden cacophony of loud voices as the warehouse rooftop flooded with armed police. The wailing sound of ambulance sirens seemed to be coming from all directions, adding to the intensity of the moment.

'If only you knew how much I loved you,' Cornish said, as he carried Melanie towards the helicopter, quite oblivious to the turmoil unfolding behind him.

Chapter 19

WE HAVE THE TRUTH

Metropolitan Police Headquarters, Victoria Embankment, Wednesday, May 8

Chief Superintendent Montgomery greeted

Alan Cornish with a broad smile and a firm handshake. The tall thick-set man with Buddy Holly style glasses and wavy, dark hair gestured with his hand and said:

'Come in and take a seat, Alan... Thanks for coming in today and good work by the way, for wrapping this nasty mess up so quickly.'

Wrapping this nasty mess up, thought Cornish. *What's he talking about?* Alan Cornish was about to respond but Superintendent Montgomery raised his hand. 'Please—sit down.'

Cornish watched as the uniformed superintendent settled into his swivel chair behind his large, leather-topped desk.

'Thanks to you and your team, Alan, I can now hand this case back to Ronnie Jarvis for him to close. Very well done!'

Cornish looked astounded.

Montgomery continued:

'The report will state that the two perpetrators of the break-in and murders at Broadwick Street were identified and apprehended during an armed confrontation at the warehouse. Both assailants were shot dead by armed police officers during the confrontation.' Montgomery smiled. 'As far as I'm concerned the case is closed.'

Cornish spoke:

'But we don't know for sure if it was them who killed the Russian and his girlfriend.'

'The evidence is overwhelming, Alan. Ballistics has confirmed that the gun at the warehouse was the same one that killed the Russian. What more evidence do you want? Let's not complicate things. As far as the general public are concerned, we got the culprits. Let's just leave it like that, shall we?'

This is a stitch up. 'We need to wait, sir.'

'Wait? For what?'

'We have a young man fighting for his life in hospital. He might not survive his injuries, but if he does, and he's able to talk, then we just might get to the truth.'

Montgomery sighed despondently. 'We have the truth! The public are an impatient bunch, Alan. They don't like waiting. As far as I'm concerned this case is closed.'

Cornish knew he was not going to change this man's mind. He stood up and said:

'I would like, for the record, sir, to state that I am not satisfied with the outcome of this case. I believe it has been closed prematurely.'

Montgomery smiled and checked his watch. 'I've noted your comments, Alan... and now, I'm sorry, but I need to close this meeting. It's a busy day for me today, I'm sure you understand. Once again, thank you for your efforts.' The superintendent stood up and offered Cornish his hand. 'We'll settle your account within ninety days—our usual terms. Can you see yourself out please?'

Moments later Cornish walked out of the police headquarters onto the Victoria Embankment; his fists were clenched and his knuckles were white as he turned right and headed towards the Houses of Parliament.

Justice! What an arrogant bastard! I just hope this kid lives to tell the truth and embarrass him. He's nothing but a glory hunter looking for quick answers and jumping to conclusions simply to appease Joe Public. There's more to this case—I know it—and they know it. I can't give up on this now because there are too many unanswered questions.

With that, he took out his mobile and dialled St Thomas' Hospital where Sami Karam lay, in an induced coma, in a room guarded by two armed police officers.

The report sheet clipped to the front of the young Muslim's bed contained a note from the night nurse saying that, during the early hours of the morning, the patient showed signs of spasmodic muscular fasciculation in the fingers of both hands, which lasted for approximately ten minutes.

Chapter 20

WHAT DOESN'T KILL ME

'Are you sure you're up to this?'

Melanie smiled as she served Cornish scrambled eggs and bacon. 'How many times do I have to tell you? I'm *fine*. I really need to get back to work, love.'

'Okay, okay!'

'My neck has healed, I've had my trauma counselling and I feel *fine*,—so why not?'

Cornish leaned over his breakfast to read the front page of the Daily Telegraph laid flat in front of him on the breakfast table, and muttered something to himself. Then he looked up and said:

'...As long as *you* feel up to it then I see no reason why you should't come back to work.'

Melanie kissed the top of his head. 'I know it was traumatic for me watching that lad being thrown off the building and seeing those dead bodies but what doesn't kill me makes me stronger.'

Cornish had always admired Melanie's fighting spirit. She was not one to be beaten or one to give up easily.

'And remember in future, if I tell not to go in alone don't do it. You could have so easily been killed, Mel!'

'Yes,—I know, I went in because I wanted to save his life by talking to him—he was suicidal. I'd do the same thing again under similar circumstances. I'm sorry.'

Cornish smiled, 'I think you are ready to come back.'

'Is there any news about Sami Karam? Will he survive?' she asked.

'I *bloody* hope so, love. He's still in a medically induced coma but the consultant neurologist who operated on him is very confident that he will pull through. They intend to bring him around at the end of the week. To be honest, it's nothing short of a miracle that he's still alive. The bullet shattered part of his skull, but thankfully it didn't enter his brain, and his fall from the top of the warehouse was partially cushioned because he landed in a skip full of rubbish! What's the chances of that? Obviously Allah wasn't ready for him! Saying that though, he suffered two broken legs, a broken sternum, broken wrist and they think he might lose a kidney. But, if he is able to talk, he might just tell us what the *hell* is going on—because right now

—I don't have a clue—and the Metropolitan Police have issued a statement via SIO Ronnie Jarvis—'

'Not that *prick?*' Melanie interjected.

Cornish chuckled and continued:

'…As I said, they've issued a statement saying the two men killed at the warehouse were responsible for the murders at Broadwick Street, based on the forensic evidence that the gun fired at Sami Karam was the same gun that killed the Russian and his girl friend. So the case is now closed and Superintendent Montgomery is a very happy chappy.'

'…I thought you were the SIO?'

Cornish raised his index finger. 'Very good point! So did I,' he replied, before finishing the last morsel of his breakfast.

'Will there be an enquiry into the shootings at the warehouse?'

'No mention of it as yet. I think the police response was justified. After all,. they were facing two armed assailants who'd already shot one person and were threatening to cut your throat!'

Melanie subconsciously raised her hand to her neck.

Cornish continued:

'The great British public will show no sympathy towards a couple of *murderous* jihadis who were shot dead on the streets of London.'

Melanie shivered as vague images of the incident and the feeling of the cold, steel blade pressing into her neck flashed into her mind. '… It doesn't help their case does it? The gun, I mean.'

'I know—but that in itself is not enough to *prove* their guilt. Why didn't they shoot the girl as well?'

'Maybe they wanted her to suffer? Punishment for relinquishing her Muslim faith?'

Cornish became pensive and tapped his fingertips together… 'Things are not what they seem, Melanie.'

'What do mean by that?'

'Zeezee found out that the CCTV footage at Broadwick Street had been tampered with and a loop had been inserted around the time of the murders. And another thing, they found fingerprints on the gun that matched those of Jamal Karam!'

'Suggesting?'

'Firstly, to be able to tamper with the footage requires a high level of internal security and that's not something our terrorists could achieve easily.'

'And the fingerprints?' Melanie asked.

'Maybe *she* killed the Russian?'

Melanie frowned. 'What? She shot her *lover* in the head?'

'Remember Vera Parsons?'

'Yeah, good point, *Handsome*' Melanie conceded.

Cornish chuckled and stood up. 'Who knows? I'm sure I don't... Are you okay to leave for the office in about twenty minutes?' he asked, as he placed his breakfast dishes in the dishwasher.

'Of course.'

'We have a meeting in my office with Zeezee at nine-thirty to discuss communications tapes obtained from GCHQ. It appears that MI6 were listening to the Russian and his girl friend at their apartment.'

'I can't wait,' was Melanie's enthusiastic response as she headed up the stairs to get dressed.

*

When Zeezee walked into Cornish's office it was clear by his expression that something was bothering him. 'Good morning and welcome back, Melanie,' he said.

'Thank you, ZeeZee,' Melanie replied. 'It's good to be back.'

'You might change your mind when you hear what I've got to say.'

Cornish frowned. 'What's the problem, Buddy?'

'We've been *officially* cut off from GCHQ! We are no longer able to discuss the Broadwick Street murders with SIGINT—that's Signals Intelligence to you and me.'

Cornish banged his desk. 'Damn it! This is Montgomery's doing.'

Zeezee continued:

'GCHQ had been listening to Maxim Mikhailov's conversations at Broadwick Street and supplying MI6 with the tapes. Apparently MI6 has been interested in the Russian ever since he set foot in the country. I only found this out this morning, after talking to an old colleague of mine who still works for SIGINT and soon after that we were blocked!'

Cornish inhaled deeply and tapped his finger tips together. 'Obviously we're being watched too. Montgomery never mentioned the phone tap, but he must have known about it.'

'It wasn't just a phone tap, Alan, they had a pickup on one of the windows. They look like bird shit, apparently.'

'Zeezee, you know me, I'm like a dog with a bone. This whole thing stinks and I want to get to the bottom of it!'

Melanie smiled and nodded. *I feel exactly the same way,* she mused.

Zeezee smiled for the first time. 'Well,—my ole colleague can't help us any more, because from precisely nine fifteen this morning we were officially *"Sent to Coventry,"* so to speak— but it's not the end of the world.'

Cornish smiled back. 'Meaning?'

Zeezee inhaled though his teeth. '...Let's just say that I know a lot about GCHQ and their communications network, because I helped to develop their VPN and firewall protocols.'

Cornish looked intrigued. 'VPN?'

'Yeah—Virtual Private Network—It allows their closed client-server infrastructure to communicate securely through a public network like the internet for example , protected by a shell of multi-layered, encryption software.'

'Don't tell me,' interjected Melanie, 'software you helped to develop?'

'Precisely! It's used by MI6's foreign intelligence operatives —their spies.'

Cornish looked intrigued. 'What are you intimating, Zeezee?'

Zeezee donned a wide grin. '...I can still access the information we need and they won't be able to trace us. It means that effectively we're invisible!'

Melanie asked:

'How sure are you that we can do this without being found out?'

Zeezee nodded confidently. '...Very sure,' he replied.

Melanie added:

'Because if we get caught—'

'They'll shut us down!' Cornish interjected.

'Exactly!' replied Melanie. 'And lock us up and throw away the keys!'

For a few moments all three remained silent, contemplating the consequences of their possible actions.

Zeezee then broke the silence:

'It has to be *your* call, Alan.'

Cornish again glanced at Melanie, as if trying to read her thoughts, before finally looking back at Zeezee and saying:

'Let me get this right, Zeezee. You're suggesting we hack into GCHQ's communications network. The very network they use to *hack* into secret foreign intelligence agencies on a global scale?'

Zeezee nodded and smirked. 'Yeah,' he replied. 'Pretty cool, don't you think?'

Finally, Cornish said, confidently:

'…That's pretty cool. Let's do it!'

Yes! A clenched fist in Melanie's imagination punched the air and her heartbeat quickened.

That's why I love you Alan Cornish, she thought. 'Yeah—Let's do it!' she replied, and hugged Cornish.

'Hell yeah! let's do it,' replied Zeezee, hoping for a hug but not getting one.

'I think I need a strong coffee,' Cornish admitted, 'because if that is the case, Zeezee, we now have a real chance of finding out what the hell is going on!

Chapter 21

FINAL PREPARATIONS

The Dorchester Hotel, Park Lane, London; four days before the double murders at Broadwick Street

It was a bright morning when Tomas Soukal awoke from a wonderfully restful night's sleep. He yawned, checked his watch and decided to have breakfast in his room. Reluctantly, he slipped out of the enormous bed and stretched out his arms as he walked to the window, which offered views of the lush greenery of Hyde Park; but his thoughts where elsewhere because the time was fast approaching when he would assassinate the young Russian, with a bullet to the head, to fulfil his lucrative contract. But first he needed to do some more reconnaissance. He needed to finalise the details of his modus operandi. The *core* of his plan was in place, but he needed to visit the vicinity of the Russian's apartment one more time—but not before breakfast. He sauntered over to the writing desk, picked up the telephone receiver and pressed the room service button.

'Good morning—yes, I'd like to order breakfast for eight-thirty,' he said, 'I'd like fresh orange juice, *crisp* streaky bacon, two, sunny-side-up, fried eggs, sausage, black-pudding, tomatoes and mushrooms, *white* toast and strawberry jam, together with a cafetiére of *strong* coffee.'

At precisely 10.00 am Tomas Soukal arrived, on foot, at Broadwick Street. He wanted to observe the daily goings-on in the busy street. He had already collected the Amazon box that would be part of his plan on the day and he'd spoken to one of the Amazon delivery men to confirm that they worked seven-days-a-week. On two previous occasions he'd watched Maksim Mikhailov and his girlfriend leave their apartment around 8.00 am and walk past him, so close that he could have touched them, towards the underground station at Oxford Circus, and fortuitously, he'd heard Mikhailov say to his girlfriend:

"I *plan to stay in bed all day Sunday if it's a late night on Saturday.*"

Once the young assassin was happy with how and when he'd gain access to the Russian's apartment, he returned to the Dorchester for a well deserved, three-hour, spa treatment.

114

Chapter 22

NERVOUS TIMES

Alan Cornish was unusually quiet during the drive to the office and Melanie knew that he was still deep in thought.

'Are we still going ahead with it then?' she asked, as Cornish steered the Jaguar into Probe's forecourt and parked up in his slot next to the main entrance. He then turned off the car's engine, looked at Melanie and smiled nervously. 'Yeah,' he said, 'we're going ahead with it because I'm not giving up on this. Do you remember how determined you were when you were investigating Vera Parsons?'

Melanie gigged. 'Yeah, I remember,' she said.

'Well, that's how I feel about *this* case, Mel. If Montgomery didn't want us to solve this enigma then he shouldn't have taken us on in the first place! We're not quitters.'

Melanie smiled and reached over to hold his hand. 'This is high risk, Alan. You could lose *everything*.'

'Including you?'

'Oh no! You won't lose *me* that easily!'

'That's good to know,' Cornish said, as he leaned over and kissed her.

Melanie touched the end of Cornish's nose. 'I was referring to your baby. The thing you've put your heart and soul into for so long to make it so successful and so respected.'

Cornish puffed out his cheeks and replied:

'...Yes, I know—but I have *total* trust in Zeezee... Come on let's do it,' he said, enthusiastically, and exited the car. Melanie took a deep breath, exited the car, and followed Cornish into Probe's main entrance.

Zeezee was sitting at his desk sipping coffee from his favourite Gonzo mug when Cornish and Melanie joined him, both carrying steaming mugs of coffee.

'Morning, Maestro,' said Cornish, as they approached.

'Morning both,' Zeezee replied, 'grab a seat.'

Cornish and Melanie settled on chairs next to Zeezee in front of his computer screen.

'Let's do it,' Cornish said.

Zeezee smiled, turned towards the screen and said, 'Yeah—let's do it,' as his fingers danced on the keyboard.

Melanie watched as Zeezee continued to type for what seemed like an age. He then looked at Cornish and said:

'This is it, Alan.'

Cornish glanced at Melanie who forced a tight-lipped smile and then he nodded to Zeezee.

Zeezee hit a key on the keyboard. A moment later a smile lit up his face. 'We're in!' he said.

Melanie watched Cornish as he stared anxiously at the computer screen.

'Look at this,' Zeezee enthused, 'this directory contains all the classified audio tapes for the Russian's apartment.'

'Can you access them?' Cornish asked.

'Of course,' Zeezee replied, 'I developed the external security protocol myself. I'll download the audio files so we can listen to them.'

'How long have we got?' Melanie asked, nervously.

Zeezee turned and smiled at her. 'I'm connected via VPS on the Dark Web using Tor, or O*nionland,* as we call it; lots of layers, you see, like an onion—so don't worry, Melanie, they can't trace us.'

Melanie frowned. 'I've heard of it but what exactly is the Dark Web, Zeezee?'

'It's a way of accessing *encrypted* online content that your standard browser can't get at, but more importantly the user can't be identified by the authorities. And, as you'd expect, the criminal underworld love it for *that* very reason.'

Melanie let out a nervous sigh and rubbed the palms of her hands together. 'I hope you're right,' she said.

'Trust me,' Zeezee replied.

'Download them as quickly as possible, Zeezee, and then break the connection.' Cornish insisted. 'If we're not incarcerated by tomorrow we can *consider* doing it again.'

Zeezee laughed loudly. 'I'll let you know when I'm done Alan—it shouldn't take too long.'

Cornish stood up and downed the last of his coffee. Let's reconvene in my office in one hour. I can't wait to know what happened at Broadwick Street on the day they were murdered.

*

St Thomas' Hospital, London

Fourteen days after he'd been shot in the head on the roof of the warehouse in east London, Sami Karam's eyes slowly opened. The blurred image standing next to him gradually came into focus and he looked up at the smiling face of a nurse.

'Hello,' she said, 'and how are you feeling?'

'Where am I?' he replied, weakly.

'You're in hospital. You've been seriously injured; you've been in an induced coma to help your brain recover.'

He reached up to his head and touched the bandages wrapped around his skull. He then closed his eyes and inhaled deeply. 'I didn't die, he said, exhaling.'

'No—*miraculously,* you didn't die.'

'But I *wanted* to die,' he said.

'Don't say that young man. You were very *lucky* to survive your injuries. You're going to be okay.'

'No!—You don't understand.'

The nurse glanced at the spike that suddenly appeared on the heart-rate monitor display. 'Please try to stay calm,' she said.

The young Muslim stared up at the ceiling and his dark eyes welled up. '…I didn't want to live—I *wanted* to die! *Please*, let me die.'

The nurse smiled. 'I'm sorry, but I've been trained to save people's lives. You're asking the wrong person. You Muslims are all so *preoccupied* with death, when life itself is so much *more* important. Here, sip some water please,' she said, offering up the glass to his mouth.

Sami Karam ignored her request. 'You're wrong,' he snapped, 'the Qur'an prepares us for life *after* death!'

'Drink!' she insisted and this time he sipped from the glass.

'What about the innocent people killed in the name of Islam who have never read the Qur'an. Who prepares *them* for life after death? I'm sorry, but I don't believe any of that religious

119

stuff. I'm a lot older than you and I've come to realise that happiness, kindness, respect for others, freedom of speech and more compassion is what this world requires, and those things don't *need* religion for them to happen; to think they do is just a fallacy. It simply needs people to come to their senses and understand how history has played its part in manipulating the way we think. Love will bring us together—but hatred and anger will simply destroy us'…The nurse picked up the clipboard at the bottom of the bed and filled in some data. 'Do you read much, young man? I love books,' she said, realising it was time to change the subject.

'There is only one book you need to read and that book is the Qur'an.—It is the word of God, dictated to Muhammed by the archangel Gabriel.'

The nurse shook her head and tutted. 'Doesn't seem to bring you happiness though, does it?' she added with a cheesy grin. 'I think I'll stick with Victoria Hislop if that's okay with you?'

'Stick with what?'

'…Nothing, try and relax now and drink plenty of water please. I'll be back to see you shortly.'

From outside the room, one of the armed police officers had glanced through the window and noticed that Sami Karam was awake and talking to the nurse. The officer immediately dialled a number on his mobile and said:

'He's conscious, sir,——yes sir, he's talking to the nurse, ——yes sir,——I understand, sir.' The officer ended the call and looked across at the other armed officer. 'No visitors under any circumstances,' he said, checking his MP5 semi-automatic carbine.

Chapter 23

DOCTOR UNDERWOOD

Probe's Offices, Cambridge

'There are two armed guards outside Sami Karam's room and no-one is allowed in—other than hospital staff.'

'Is he talking, Tom?' Cornish asked.

'Apparently, although he is very weak and very unhappy to be alive, so I'm told.'

Cornish looked at Melanie and said:

'We need to talk to him.'

Melanie raised her eyebrows. 'And just how do you intend to do that?'

'Not me,—you!'

'Me!' Melanie exclaimed.

Cornish smirked. 'Yes, you.'

*

Melanie pushed open the double doors and walked towards Sami Karam's room. She was dressed in a white coat and carrying a clip board. She was wearing a long, black wig and wearing dark-rimmed glasses. Her ID badge was labelled *Doctor Sarah Evans—Senior Neurologist.* She smiled as she approached the two intimidating guards that were already eyeing her from head to toe. Inside her, she was fighting to control her growing anxiety; externally she looked calm and confident.

'Excuse me officer,' she said, to the armed policeman who was standing in front of the door. The policeman squinted at her badge.

'Dr Evans—Neurology Department,' she said, calmly.

The guard frowned.

'You know—brains. I need to check what he has left,' she said, glancing at his rifle.

The guard's expression remained stoic as he moved slowly to the side to allow Melanie through.

'Thank you,' she said, and opened the door into the room. 'Oh—by the way—please make sure I'm not disturbed for the next *fifteen* minutes. It's important for the test, you understand.'

'Yes, ma'am,' came the reply—a reply that made Melanie smile.

When the door closed one of guards pouted and nodded his approval.

'Yeah, very tasty,' said the other guard.

Sami Karam was awake when Melanie approached his bed. 'Hello Sami, how are you feeling today?' she said.

'…I know you,' he said, 'you were at the warehouse.'

Melanie turned to make sure the door was closed. 'Yes, that's right, Sami—that was me. I'm sorry for what happened to you. It wasn't what I had in mind.'

'Who are you?'

'My name's Melanie.'

Pointing a finger he said:

'It says Sarah on your badge!'

'Yes,—yes, I know, but it's the only way I could get to see you. I hope you don't mind?'

'Why do you want to see me?'

'Sami, I need to know why those people tried to kill you and I need to know who killed your sister and her boyfriend.'

Melanie glanced at the door. 'Will you tell me?'

'Are you from the police?' he asked.

'No, I'm a private investigator.'

The young Muslim regarded Melanie for some time. 'Did they hurt you?' he finally asked.

Melanie smiled and settled on a chair next to his bed. '…I thought I was going to die, to be honest,' she said, 'but thankfully they were killed before they could cut my throat.'

'You were lucky,' he said, 'they were rabid monsters.'

'You were lucky *too*,' Melanie replied.

Karam lowered his head. 'I wanted to die,' he said.

'But you survived and they died. You're safe now. Why did they want you dead, Sami?'

Sami Karam took a deep breath. His expression became pensive. '…Because I was a failure,' he eventually replied.

Melanie frowned. 'I don't understand.'

'How could you? You're not a *jihadi.*'

'Are you a jihadi? Did *you* kill your sister, Sami?'

Karam covered his face with his hands. '…No!—That's why I'm a *failure*. My sister became a common whore. She gave up her faith and Allah decreed that she should die for her transgressions. I was ordered to kill her.'

'Allah knew about your sister's transgressions?'

Karam ignored the question. 'I was trained to kill—but I couldn't do it…I couldn't kill a *rabbit*! I failed them and I failed Allah and my punishment was death… I went on the run so I could decide how and when to end it all. I'd planned to jump off the warehouse anyway.'

'…So did *they* kill your sister instead?'

'They both went there to kill her; to do what I couldn't.—
My sister, she—'

At that moment the door opened and a young nurse walked
in carrying a tray.

'Excuse me, Doctor, but I have to change his head dressing
before Mr Carmichael from Neurology calls in on his rounds.'

Melanie stood up. 'Yes, of course—go ahead,' she replied,
trying not to show her annoyance at being disturbed.

'You're new here, aren't you?' the nurse said, placing the
tray on the side table opposite Melanie.

Melanie smiled. 'Yes,—I recently joined Mr Carmichael's
department.'

'I thought so, because I've not seen you around.'

Melanie realised it was time to get out of there. 'I'll leave
you to it then, nurse,' she said.

'Thanks Doctor Evans, and nice to meet you,' she replied, as
Sami Karam quickly pushed the mobile phone and note that
Melanie had given him under his pillow.

When Melanie got to the main lifts the doors opened and a tall,
silver-haired man exited, followed closely by his band of
waddling, junior doctors.

Well, well, if it isn't Mr Carmichael himself, she thought,
glancing at his ID badge. She turned away and quickly decided
to take the stairs to her left; removing her ID and white coat as
she descended.

Melanie's heart was pounding as she walked out of the hospital building into bright sunshine. 'Alan Cornish, you *owe* me one,' she said to herself.

Fifteen minutes later, she was sipping a double espresso in a cafe near Westminster tube station and looking at her unfamiliar refection in the wall mirror when her mobile phone started ringing. She looked at the display, half expecting a call from Alan Cornish, but, to her surprise, it was Sami Karam calling.

'Hi Sami,' she said, 'I was hoping you'd call me.'

'…The three of them went there,' he said.

'Three?'

'Yes, you must remember, I failed, and my sister—'

'Sami?—Sami? What about your sister? What about her?— Shit! Shit! Shit!' Melanie exclaimed as the line went dead. She quickly redialled the number but there was no answer. She dialled again but there was still no answer. 'Shit!' she cried out again, despondently.

Chapter 24

BUT YOU DON'T KNOW

Melanie always talked a lot when she was nervous.

'They must know it was us, Alan?'

'Melanie, take a chill pill. They don't know it was us,' Cornish replied, as he glanced at his watch.

'So why have they called us in? I thought you said the case was closed?'

'It was and I'm not sure, but we're about to find out, my love.'

'Oh, Alan, I do hope you're right.'

So do I, Cornish thought, as they made their way into the main entrance of the Metropolitan Police Headquarters at Victoria Embankment.

At the reception desk, Cornish informed the young lady that they were there for a meeting with Chief Superintendent Montgomery.

The receptionist glanced at her screen and asked:

'Your names please?'

'Alan Cornish and Melanie Underwood, we're from Probe.'

'Yes, I've got you; your meeting is arranged for eleven o'clock.'

'That's correct,' Cornish replied, checking his watch.

The receptionist handed them an ID badge each. 'Please wear these around your neck at all times when in the building. Take the lift to the fourth floor and someone will be there to meet you, Mr Cornish.'

Cornish thanked her and they walked off towards the lifts. Melanie took Cornish's hand and squeezed it tight. 'Never a dull moment—and that's why I love you so much,' she said, as they walked.

'And that is all that matters,' he replied, with a contented grin that masked his inner turmoil.

The lift doors opened at the fourth floor and there to meet them was a uniformed Chief Superintendent Montgomery.

'Alan, good of you to come,' he said, offering his hand.

'This is my colleague, Melanie Underwood,' Cornish replied, after shaking hands.

Melanie then shook hands with Montgomery and he said:

'Welcome to the Met. Is this your first visit here, Miss Underwood?'

'Yes, it is,' she replied, trying to remain calm.

Montgomery gestured to them to enter his office and when they walked in they noticed a man standing at the window looking out at the view.

Montgomery said:

'I'd like to introduce you to Neil Bartholomew,' as the middle-aged man dressed in a tailored, black suit turned to face them. His wavy, straw coloured hair was cut short at the back and sides and he wore round, gold-rimmed glasses. He walked forward to shake Cornish's hand. 'Nice to meet you Mr Cornish,' he said, with a public school accent and then he simply smiled at Melanie before saying:

'Your face is vaguely familiar, Miss Underwood, do I know you?'

'Not that I'm aware of, Mr Bartholomew, she replied.'

That's a bad start, she thought, *he's recognised me from the hospital CCTV footage!*

Montgomery gestured to Cornish and Melanie to sit on chairs in front of his desk as he and Neil Bartholomew settled on seats behind the large, leather-topped desk.

Deliberately intimidating, Cornish thought. *Who is this guy?*

Montgomery fidgeted nervously with his fountain pen.

What's going on, Cornish mused?

Once everyone was settled, Montgomery said:

'Neil is from MI6.'

Oh fuck! Cornish's mind immediately went into overdrive.

Neil Bartholomew smiled, insipidly, and then said:

'As you probably know Mr Cornish, MI6 works very closely with GCHQ.'

Oh fuck! They've got us! Melanie thought.

'I'd be very surprised if it didn't,' Cornish retorted.

'Yes, precisely,' replied Bartholomew, with an insipid smile that Melanie found quite intimidating.

He continued:

'And we *know* that your organisation has deliberately hacked into GCHQ.'

Cornish sat upright and looked the man from MI6 in the eyes. '…Actually, you *don't* know that, Mr Bartholomew,' he replied, coolly.

Bartholomew smiled again. 'Very sure of yourself, aren't you, Mr Cornish?'

'Very sure, Mr Bartholomew.'

The man from MI6 huffed then looked straight at Melanie again. 'We also believe that your organisation has talked, without permission, to Sami Karam.'

Melanie's expression remained impassive.

'But you can't prove that, either,' Cornish added.

Montgomery shifted uneasily in his seat and glanced at Bartholomew, who continued to maintain a relaxed demeanour.

Bartholomew then rubbed his chin pensively before saying:

'It appears that we underestimated the resolve of your organisation, Mr Cornish.'

Alan Cornish allowed himself a wry smile.

Bartholomew continued. 'You believe that the murders were not committed by the Islamists, don't you?'

'I think the case is more complicated than that.'

'So—do you know who killed them?'

'No, we genuinely don't know.'

'I appreciate your honesty.' Bartholomew stood up and walked over to the window again. Looking out, with his back to them, he said:

'I want to offer you a deal, Mr Cornish.'

What the fuck! thought Melanie.

'What kind of a deal, Mr Bartholomew?' Cornish asked.

'A deal potentially worth a lot of money to Probe; we're happy to double your outrageous rate, just as long as you're prepared to not rock the boat.'

Cornish frowned and Montgomery lowered his head.

'Please, let me explain,' Bartholomew continued. 'Whether the so-called jihadis did or didn't commit the murders is not important in the grand scheme of things—and they aren't here to face their punishment now anyway. The British public don't need to know the truth in this instant. They're happy with what they've already been told.'

Cornish was about to comment but Bartholomew raised his hand and quickly continued. 'But, what is *important* is the *security* of this country and the need to find out, for sure, who actually killed them and why. We believe they were both killed by Russian agents because they were foolishly attempting to sell top-secret, Russian, military information to Iran. We want you and your organisation to find out the truth. MI6 will co-operate with you—fully; you have my word. The information the Russian was going to sell to Iran was, we believe, genuine. MI6 took the decision to stop any of that sensitive information getting into the hands of our enemies. Audio tapes were made by the two of them and they intended to sell the information on USB sticks hidden in the frames of ten oil paintings. Thankfully, we now have those audio tapes in our possession.' Bartholomew smiled, 'and now, with your help, all we need to do is identify who killed the Russian.'

Cornish frowned. 'Are you not interested to know who killed the girl anymore?'

'Let's just say,' Mr Cornish, 'that would be the icing on the cake; but we presume she was killed for her involvement with the Russian.'

'That doesn't make sense. If that was the case she would have been shot too!'

Bartholomew simply raised his eyebrows.

'Can we expect full access to the *unadulterated* Broadwick Street CCTV tapes?'

'…Yes, of course.'

'…And what if we don't co-operate with your wishes and your *twisted* form of justice?' Cornish asked.

Bartholomew looked at Montgomery and smiled. He then looked back at Cornish and said:

'I think you already know the answer to that question, Mr Cornish.'

You bastard! Melanie thought.

'Oh, and one more thing before I forget,' Bartholomew donned his insipid smile again, 'no more hacking into GCHQ because that's illegal and quite frankly, it's *fucking* embarrassing to the authorities!'

Cornish returned the smile.

Fifteen minutes later

Cornish and Melanie walked out of the Metropolitan Police building and headed towards Westminster. Melanie slipped her arm into Cornish's as they walked.

'He gave me the creeps,' Melanie said, what a *pompous* bastard he was!

'Well,… at least we're not banged up in the Tower of London, accused of treason,' Cornish replied.

'But it appears that we've got ourselves in a bit of a corner, doesn't it, Alan?'

'Yes, it does, doesn't it.'

'What do you intend to do then?'

'I intend to buy us some delicious Danish pastries and some strong coffee.'

Melanie put her arm around Cornish and kissed him. 'Good idea,' she said.

Their conversation continued in the coffee shop

Cornish sipped his extra strong latte and said:

'If I'm really honest, I don't think we have any other choice than to go along with this. They could make life very difficult for us if they wanted to.'

'Do you think they were killed by Russian agents?'

'It's most likely, isn't it? After all Mikhailov was intending to sell top-secret, Russian, military information to Iran.'

Melanie wiped cream from her top lip. 'Why Iran?' she asked.

'Well, I presume they thought Iran would be willing to pay the *most* money for the information.'

Melanie considered his response for a moment. 'So do you think Iran got the information from Mikhailov?'

'That's a very good question. I believe MI6 know far more than they are admitting to, and I cannot imaging them allowing information that sensitive to get into the hands of the Iranian Revolutionary Guard. MI6 has been involved in this from the very beginning; ever since Mikhailov came to the UK.'

'Do you think they'll co-operate with us?'

'We'll do whatever we have to do to get this case off our backs—with or without their co-operation, my love. But I don't see the benefit to them of not co-operating with us—unless they're playing a game with us and I don't understand the rules.'

'When he offered to pay us *double* our rate, it felt like they were buying our silence.'

Cornish downed the remains of his coffee. 'My thoughts exactly! But this is bigger than money—this is international politics and now we are *stuck* in the middle, like an angry and wounded bull being taunted by a sanguine matador!'

Melanie forced a weak smile. 'Sometimes the bull wins,' she suggested.

Cornish looked into her eyes. 'That's good, because I don't fancy having my balls cut off!'

'Don't worry darling—I won't let that happen,' Melanie said, with a giggle, 'As you know, I'm very fond of your balls.'

At that moment Cornish's phone rang. 'Yes, Tom?' he said, and listened in silence for a few moments before saying:

'…Okay, thanks,—we'll see you back at the office after lunch. We can discuss it more then.'

Melanie guessed from Cornish's downbeat tone that it wasn't good news. 'What's happened now?'

'Sami Karam.'

'What about him?'

'He died an hour ago!'

Melanie sighed. '…Now we'll never know who the third person was?'

'We might! We need to see the CCTV footage that Bartholomew promised us, remember? That might answer a few questions,' Cornish suggested. 'I'll get Zeezee on to it,' he said, dialling the office.

Chapter 25

A LATE DELIVERY

The Dorchester Hotel, Sunday evening, 5 May

Tomas Soukal's hands were rock steady as he filled the special dart from a syringe that contained a knockout cocktail of powerful drugs. When he was satisfied that all the air bubbles were expelled from the glass capsule on the dart, he repeated the exercise on another spare dart that he hoped he wouldn't need. On his bed was the Amazon box with the cut-out bottom and his Glock 9mm pistol and silencer. He checked his false beard in the bathroom mirror and donned a pair of black-framed glasses and a green, beanie hat.

'You look just like him,' he said to himself, checking the image on his phone of a regular delivery man to Broadwick Street. He then screwed the silencer onto his pistol and placed it in his backpack along with the spare dart that he fitted into a protective plastic tube. He carefully loaded the air pistol with the first dart and placed the Amazon box over the top. 'Not your average delivery, Tomas,' he said, and laughed. 'Time to go.'

It was ten-thirty when he arrived at Broadwick Street. The evening was unusually warm and the place was reasonably quiet, apart from a singer's voice in the nearby pub belting out a classic Irish folksong that the young assassin didn't recognise.

Carrying the Amazon box with the air pistol hidden inside, he walked up to the illuminated doorbells at the front of the building, pressed the second one down and waited. A moment later a female voice said, 'Hello.'

'Amazon late delivery for you, Miss Karam,' he said. There was a clunking noise and he knew the front door was open. He entered the building and walked up the stairs. As he reached the second floor apartment, the door opened and Jamal Karam appeared in the doorway, smiling; music was playing in the apartment.

'You're late tonight?' she said.

'Yeah, sorry,' he said, 'I've been really busy today.'

'I didn't get a text to say you were coming. Is it for me or Max?' Jamal asked, excitedly.

The delivery man walked up to her with the ubiquitous Amazon box in front of him and said:

'This one is for you.' There was a muffled hiss when he squeezed the trigger. Jamal jolted backwards, cringed and lifted her hand to the point of sudden pain in her neck. Immediately her eyes started to roll and she collapsed on the floor as her legs buckled beneath her.

'What have you bought now?' came a despairing voice from somewhere to the left, within the apartment.

Tomas Soukal quietly closed the front door. Carefully stepping over Jamal, he walked in the direction of the voice, pulling the Glock out of his backpack as he did.

'What have you bought?' came the voice again.

Got you, he thought, before kicking the door open to see a startled Maksim Mikhailov relaxing in a hot, foaming bath.

'Who the *fuck* are you?' the Russian cried out.

The assassin coolly pointed his Glock at Maksim Mikhailov's head and fired off just one round. He then watched, unemotionally, as splattered blood and brain tissue trickled down the tiles behind his victim's shattered skull.

He then walked calmly back into the lounge, grabbed Jamal by the ankles and dragged her onto the large, white rug in the middle of the room. Next, he methodically unscrewed the silencer and dropped it into his backpack, before wiping the gun clean and placing it in her hand. Kneeling down next to her he gently stroked her raven-black hair and ran his latex covered fingers over her voluptuous breasts.

'What a beautiful creature you are,' he said, 'killing you would be such a waste.' He then extracted the dart from her neck. 'Sorry about your boyfriend,' he whispered, 'but it's nothing personal you understand.'

The young assassin gathered his things and glanced around the room before walking out of the apartment and closing the door behind him. He wasn't aware of the audio tapes Jamal and Mikhailov had made over a period of four days, as they fed the ducks in Hyde Park, describing the details of the Russian top-secret establishments; but they had been taken from the apartment earlier in the day anyway.

Tomas Soukal had already worked out the best route, by foot, back to the hotel. A route with the minimum number of CCTV cameras to worry about and a large selection of bins on route to dispose of his beard, glasses and hat.

Within an hour of killing Maksim Mikhailov he'd taken a long, hot shower and was relaxing in bed watching the late-night news; knowing that tomorrow he would leave London, pick up his Mercedes in Croydon and drive back to Germany for a few days of sexual debauchery in Hamburg; before returning to Prague to collect the final payment of fifty-thousand US dollars in cash from his latest employer. As he lay in bed he wondered whether he should have taken the Amazon box with him and not left it in the apartment. It didn't matter.

Chapter 26

NOT YOUR AVERAGE ASSASSIN

Probe's Offices, Cambridge

'So what's the latest, Tom?' Cornish asked as he carefully carried a tray of steaming coffee mugs into his office.

Tom Weiss was sitting at the round table, together with Melanie and Zeezee. '…Well, it appears that he died in his sleep,' he replied, 'they tried to resuscitate him but obviously that didn't work.'

Melanie picked up one of the coffee mugs and took a sip. 'I don't think he wanted to live,' she added, helping herself to a chocolate Hobnob from a plate on the table.

'No foul play then, Tom?' Cornish asked as he settled on to a chair at the table.

Tom Weiss shook his head. 'No, I really don't think so, Alan. As we know, access was restricted to medical staff only and the room was guarded twenty-four-hours-a-day; I know first-hand how hard it was, because I tried to visit him.'

Cornish glanced at Melanie and smiled. 'Unless you're Dr Evans from Neurology of course.'

Tom Weiss chuckled, Melanie grinned and then replied:
'I was so nervous,' she stressed, as she took another biscuit from the plate. 'Those armed police are quite intimidating, the way they look at you… I think I could be an actor, you know!'

Weiss added:

'Confucius say, one pretty smile is worth a thousand keys,' as he also helped himself to a biscuit.

'Are you sure he said that?' Cornish asked, jokingly.

'Not really,' Weiss replied, 'but it sounded good didn't it?'

And they all dissolved into laughter.

Cornish sipped his coffee and then turned his attention to the matters at hand. Looking at Zeezee, he said:

'Okay, let's get down to business… Did MI6 keep their promise about the CCTV tapes?'

Zeezee smiled. 'Yes, they did.'

Cornish raised his eyebrows and asked:

'So do we now know who committed the murders?'

Zeezee sniggered. 'I wish it was that easy, Alan,' he said, as he opened his laptop, 'but we now have a better idea of who visited the apartments. On the Sunday night we have the comings and goings of the residents and one late-evening visit by a delivery driver carrying an Amazon box . He's a regular visitor to the area, so I don't think he's a suspect in any of this.' Zeezee leaned forward and started the CCTV video images of the Sunday evening at Broadwick Street.

Cornish and Melanie watched the speeded up images of people walking past the apartments and the occasional person leaving or entering the property.

'We've checked them out,' Zeezee said, 'they're all genuine residents.'

As the timeline reached 10.30 the delivery man appeared and walked up to the front door of the apartment carrying an Amazon box. Melanie leaned forward with sudden interest and watched as he entered. Four minutes later he exited the building and walked away.

Melanie asked:

'Can you go back to where he enters the building and stop the video?'

Zeezee obliged and Melanie sat in silence staring at the image on the screen.

'What is it?' Cornish asked.

For a moment Melanie remained silent and pensive. 'It may be nothing,' she finally replied, 'but that box was in the apartment.'

'So we know for sure that he delivered the box to the Russian,' Zeezee added, 'which means they were still alive at that time of the evening.'

'Yes, but I noticed something strange about it. It had the back and base of the box cut away; as if the box was designed to be hiding something underneath.'

'Like a gun?!' replied Cornish.

'...Are we looking at the killer?' Zeezee asked, inquisitively, before shaking his head. '...No! Not your local delivery man!'

'He doesn't look like your *archetypal* assassin, I must admit, Zeezee,' Cornish agreed, as he stood up and walked over to his desk. 'Melanie,—let's get this guy in for questioning *immediately*, so that we can eliminate him from our enquires.'

Melanie nodded. 'Will do... By the way, Alan, I also want to question the cleaning lady again, now that she's had time to calm down.'

Cornish looked mildly surprised. 'Umm—are you suggesting that she might be involved in all of this, after all?'

'...I just want to be sure that she's told us *everything* that happened that morning.'

Cornish smiled. 'Okay,—do it,' he said, and settled into his captain's chair.

'I'm on to it,' Melanie replied and walked out of the office.

....*She's on to something,* Cornish mused, tapping his fingertips together. Then he picked up the phone to request a warrant and an armed response unit from the Met.

Chapter 27

UNINVITED VISITORS

London's East End

Like so many young, ambitious Albanians, Tarik Hasani dreamt of a better life. His country, situated on the Balkan Peninsula and still suffering economically from the aftermath of communism, sadly offered little hope of a good life for its rising generation. So, three years ago he uprooted and left Albania for good, promising his aged father that he would soon return home with money to spend. His promises fell on deaf ears and a year later his father died, a sad and lonely man.

But that was then. Now, he was finally making money, not a lot, but the future was definitely brighter, living and working in London. His little, one room bedsit was tiny. Welcome light came in through a single, slanted window in the ceiling and the only way he could wash was at the small, white, enamel sink in the corner of the room. There was a single bed, an uncomfortable brown, faux-leather sofa and a small IKEA dresser and chair where he placed his laptop. The room was cramped and depressing and his twice-a-week shower at the local swimming pool on Sunday and Wednesday evenings was something he relished.

Now that Amazon Prime was available in central London he was busy, very busy, delivering the ubiquitous brown boxes all over the city. He needed to be busy, to repay the money he borrowed to set himself up. If he didn't repay the Albanian drug gang in full he knew that they would kill him.

Motivated, Tarik checked his appearance in the wall mirror. He smoothed his ever thickening, black beard and pushed his black-rimmed glasses up onto the bridge of his nose before donning his beanie hat.

'Time to earn some money,' he said, to his reflection. As he turned there was a loud knock on the door. Nobody had ever knocked his door before and the penetrating sound unsettled him.

'Who is it?' he said, nervously. Then came a second loud knock. The young Albanian froze, not knowing what to do. A moment later there was a deafening bang as his door flung open and two armed police, wielding rifles, entered, shouting:

'Get down, get down on the floor now!'

Confused and petrified to the spot, the young Albanian was forced to the floor by one of the officers while the other searched the room for weapons.

'All clear,' came the ensuing instruction as they walked out of the room to allow Alan Cornish and Melanie Underwood in.

'Please get up,' Cornish said, as he and Melanie entered the room.

The young Albanian got to his feet and stared incredulously at the two uninvited visitors invading his space.

'What is the fuck is happening?' he asked, nervously, as he adjusted his beanie hat and steadied himself.

*

Later at Probe's Offices

Standing in the kitchenette, Cornish helped himself to a slice of pizza from a box on the worktop. 'So it wasn't him, his story checks out. At the time we thought he was visiting the Russian's apartment, he was actually at a Kebab house having his usual Sunday night *feast*, as he called it. Amazon confirmed that he never works on a Sunday. It's his one-day-a-week off! His routine is to visit the local swimming pool, early evening, for a shower and then go for a meal afterwards.'

'Everything checks out,' added Tom Weiss. 'I spoke with the owner of the Kebab House. He said he's a regular there and was definitely at the Kebab house the night of the murders. He confirmed that he left about eleven fifteen.'

Cornish nodded in agreement. 'The killer is clever, very clever. I suggest he went to the trouble of looking like this Albanian guy to disguise his own identity and to gain easy access to the property. So he's either a local or someone who recced the place beforehand—like a professional assassin. I would suggest his backpack carried the Glock that killed the Russian. The same gun used by our dead jihadis, which means they must have arrived at the apartment *after* the Russian had been assassinated and found the gun there; but an assassin would not normally leave his weapon at the scene of a crime, unless it was to frame someone else.'

Tom Weiss responded:

'I agree.'

'So when they arrived at the apartment, Jamal Karam *must* have been still alive; so why didn't she call the police?' responded Melanie.

Cornish sipped his coffee pensively and finally he said:

'Most likely it was our assassin that tied her to the chair. But if that's the case, then who let them into the apartment?'…

'Maybe the assassin didn't bother to close the door when he left?' suggested Melanie.

Cornish nodded in agreement. 'That's very possible. We need to get that Amazon box over to Copeland and Associates for Christopher to work his magic.'

Melanie nodded. 'And I need to talk to the cleaning lady, Miss Halabi, again. I'm expecting her and the interpreter in twenty minutes,' she said, glancing at her watch.

'Good luck with that one,' Cornish replied, as he washed his hands in the kitchen sink; after devouring another slice of pizza.

'No stone unturned,' Melanie replied with a smile, and headed back to her desk.

Cornish became quietly pensive. Finally, he looked at Tom Weiss and said:

'Our assassin was out to kill the Russian. We know from the CCTV footage that he certainly didn't have time to decapitate them. Melanie was right—that must have been done by someone else.'

Weiss rubbed his leathery chin and nodded slowly in agreement.

'This is turning into a *motherfucker* of a murder case, boss,' he replied.

'Yeah! Let's go and see Zeezee and look at the CCTV footage again.'

'I'm not sure what game MI6 is playing, Alan,' Zeezee said, as he turned away from his computer screen to face his colleagues.

'What are the bastards up to now?' responded Cornish, with a frown.

'I've just received *another* version of the CCTV video files from MI6 for the days around the time of the murders, with an apology, would you believe, saying that we were sent the *wrong* version'!

Tom Weiss looked at Cornish in astonishment. 'How many versions of the *truth* do they have for fuck's sake?'

'Good question,' replied Zeezee.

'You're right Zeezee, someone is playing games with us. So how is this file different?' Cornish asked.

'I don't know yet, Alan. Let's take a look shall we?' was Zeezee's reply.

Zeezee turned to face the screen and deftly accessed the new video file.

'Go from ten-thirty Sunday night, when the delivery man arrives,' Cornish instructed.

The three of them watched the screen intently as the delivery man duly arrived with his Amazon box and minutes later left, empty handed.

'That's exactly as before,' commented Tom Weiss.

They continued to watch and their patience was rewarded when, at two-twenty-two in the morning, two men and a woman, wearing a black burka, arrived at the building and entered the front door. Forty-two minutes later, the same three people exited the building and walked briskly away.

'Where the fuck did they suddenly appear from?' exclaimed Tom Weiss. 'They weren't on the previous tape!'

Cornish leaned closer to the screen. 'I would say that's our two jihadis all right, but who the hell is the woman wearing the burka?'

'They entered the building as if they lived there,' Zeezee added. 'This is an insider job, Alan! It *must* be them who decapitated the girl.'

Cornish stood up and said:

'And the *dead* Russian too—for some reason! …We need to find that woman if we're ever going to solve this enigma.'

Tom Weiss raised his eyebrows and pouted his bottom lip in an expression of doubt. Pointing at the image on the screen he said:

'Finding *that* woman is not going to be easy, boss.'

Cornish sighed heavily and said:

'…I know Tom,—but before we get too despondent, can I suggest we wait and see what Melanie and Christopher Copeland come up with.'

Chapter 28

AN AMAZON BOX?

'I'm a bit miffed to be honest, Alan.'

'I'm not surprised, my love,' Cornish replied as he parked his Jaguar in one of the visitor slots outside the offices of the independent forensic experts, Copeland and Associates.

'I can understand the interpreter coming down with a cold but to phone me ten minutes before the meeting to cancel is just not acceptable!' Melanie flipped down the sun-visor and checked her makeup in the vanity mirror.

'Have you rearranged the meeting?' Cornish asked.

'No, not yet. I've requested it asap and I'm waiting to hear back.'

'Okay, just keep at them. Make yourself a nuisance if necessary.'

'I'm good at that,' Melanie replied with a smile. 'How do I look?'

'Beautiful—as always.'

Melanie leaned across and kissed Cornish on the lips. 'That colour suits you,' she said, and quickly exited the car.

Cornish grabbed a tissue and wiped his lips. 'I can't let Christopher think I'm a cross-dresser now, can I?' he said, getting out of the car.

Melanie laughed. 'You could never be a woman, darling.'

'That's good to know,' replied Cornish, as he opened the car's boot and picked up the plastic evidence bag that contained the Amazon box. 'I wonder what secrets this little box holds?'

Christopher Copeland listened with interest as Cornish explained the details of the double murder. On the meeting table was a pot of loose-leaf tea, white china tea cups and the compulsory chocolate Hobnob biscuits. The Amazon box had already been taken to the lab for forensic examination and the results were promised for that afternoon.

Copeland leaned forward and took his second Hobnob. 'So you think the killer used the box to cover up his gun?'

'Yeah. We think he did.' Melanie replied.

'And you say the girl had high levels of the anaesthetic, thiopental, in her blood?'

'Yes, she did, but we don't know who administered it.' Melanie replied.

'That's not a bad idea if you're about to have your head cut off,' Copeland suggested, with a hint of sarcasm.

Melanie shivered as the waxen image of the girl's severed head flashed into her mind.

'It was like a waxworks horror show, Christopher.'

'I'm sure it was, Alan. Not your average murder is it?'

Melanie smiled through tight lips. 'I'll be happy if I never have to witness anything like that again.'

At that moment the phone on the desk started ringing. Copeland picked up the receiver and said:

'Copeland speaking.'

There was a silent pause as he listened to the caller. A few moments later he replaced the receiver... Rubbing his chin and looking at Cornish he said:

'Now that—my dear friend—is *very* interesting!'

Cornish immediately sat upright, expectantly. 'What is interesting, Christopher?'

Chapter 29

THAT MAKES SENSE

'There is no evidence to suggest that the Glock was fired from the box—but—there was a hole in the front of the box where we identified the kind of fibres used by air pistol darts! And what do you know?—We found traces of thiopental around the exit hole as well.'

Cornish looked at Melanie and said:

'So he shot her first with an airgun dart and then he killed the Russian.'

'That makes sense,' Melanie replied. 'How long would she have been unconscious for, Christopher?'

Copeland glanced at his notepad. 'If it's any consolation Melanie, the young girl would still have been unconscious when they decapitated her.'

Melanie sighed. 'A small mercy, I guess,' she replied with irony in her voice.

'Could you identify the manufacturer of the darts from the fibres on the box, Christopher?'

'Possibly, Alan; we'll do our best.'

'Believe me, we need all the help we can get at the moment.'

Copeland's face framed a look of confusion. 'So is this gunman a lone wolf? I mean, he's not suspected of the decapitations as well, is he?'

Cornish shook his head. 'No, he's not. We now believe that the murder of the Russian is unrelated to the murder of his girlfriend. Our initial reaction was different of course, but the one thing that we always found confusing was the fact that he'd been shot in head and then decapitated afterwards. And to be honest with you, we still don't know the reason why. But now we have a number of suspects for the decapitations. Unfortunately, two of them are now dead.'

'Really! You're referring to the two jihadis on the roof of the warehouse?'

'Exactly!'

Melanie responded:

'We suspect it was an honour killing. You know, for relinquishing the Muslim faith.'

'And that is a sure catalyst to awaken the wrath of Allah! Fucking religion! …Pardon my French, dear. Small minded people living in the past—and riddled with hatred.'

Melanie smiled her acceptance at Copeland.

'Spoken like a true scientist, Christopher,' Cornish added with an amused chuckle.

Copeland laughed. 'Do you know how religion has shaped our society, Alan?'

Cornish smiled and humoured his friend. 'No, tell me about it, Christopher?'

'I'll tell you, Alan. Religion has taken—no, stolen—basic human emotions like love, compassion, understanding, tolerance and empathy and claimed them all for itself. Then religion replaced them and indoctrinated its faithful followers with new emotions like: fear, guilt, intolerance and *unquestioning*, unconditional devotion. The result, my friends, is the world we now live in!'

'I suspect you didn't go to church last Sunday, Christopher?' Cornish added.

Copeland laughed out loud.

Melanie's mobile vibrated in her pocket and she took it out to read the screen message from Rachel, their secretary. Looking at Cornish she said:

'The cleaning lady and an interpreter are on the way to our offices!'

Cornish raised his eyes and tutted. 'Christoper we need to go. Thank you for your help today. I'm sure you'll have your bill in the post before my arse hits the seat of the car!'

Copeland laughed again. 'We'll let you know about the dart a.s.a.p.'

'Thank you, I appreciate it,' Cornish replied.

Cornish and Melanie waved their goodbyes to Christopher Copeland, who was waving from outside the office entrance as they drove off.

'That was a timely call,' Cornish suggested, 'because believe me—he was going off on one!'

Melanie giggled. 'I do like him though.'

'He's a brilliant scientist with strong opinions.'

'And he's added a few more pieces to the jigsaw, hasn't he Alan?'

'Yeah, very slowly this enigma is beginning to unfold.'

'Let's hope the cleaning lady is as helpful as Christopher Copeland.'

'That's asking a lot, my love.'

A smile wrinkled Melanie's nose. 'Yeah, I know,' she replied, pulling out her iPad from her handbag. 'I need to read my meeting notes from the first interview again.'

'So am I right in assuming that you think she's withholding vital information?'

'…Possibly,' Melanie replied, tapping his thigh.

'Keeping your cards close to your chest, are we?'

'For the moment, my love.'

Chapter 30

THE PROVERBIAL NEEDLE IN A HAYSTACK

Probe's Offices, Cambridge

Melanie smiled at the smartly dressed man sitting opposite her who'd introduced himself as Ashraf Mohammed. A spectacled, leathery-skinned solicitor, originally from Egypt, representing his client, Miss Halabi, who was sitting quietly next to him at the table. Sitting to his right was a young, fresh-faced, faired-haired, male interpreter by the name of Hugo Constantine. The young man had already apologised for the unfortunate cancelation earlier in the day and his attitude was refreshingly bright, thought Melanie.

Having completed the introductions for the benefit of the audio tape, which included Alan Cornish, who was standing at the back of the room, Melanie began:

'It is necessary to inform Miss Halabi that the enquiry into the double murders at Broadwick Street is still ongoing and therefore she is still considered as a *possible* suspect.'

'That is why I am here,' replied her solicitor.

'I understand that, but it would have been courteous of you to inform us of your intended presence at the meeting, Mr Mohammed.'

Nice one girl, thought Cornish.

The solicitor simply raised an eyebrow but did not reply to Melanie's comment. Instead, he asked if there was any incriminating evidence against his client.

Melanie smiled weakly. 'We are not currently pursuing any line of action against your client, Mr Mohammed, other than the early stages of *possible* deportation, as she is an illegal immigrant. We simply want to make sure we have all of the facts available to us.'

Ooooh, steady girl. That's stretching the truth a bit too far! Cornish rubbed his nose nervously.

The solicitor took a sharp intake of breath. 'But she has already told you everything at the first meeting,' he replied, in a more conciliatory tone.

'I don't believe that,' Melanie responded, emphatically.

Mr Mohammed then spoke to his client in Arabic for a few moments and in response an angst expression, partially shrouded by her black hijab, exacerbated her already wretched features. She raised her hands to her mouth and tears welled up in her sad, dark-as-night, eyes.

The interpreter then spoke to Melanie:

Mr Mohammed has informed her of the deportation proceedings.

Melanie nodded in acknowledge and added:

'But—if Miss Halabi choses to be fully co-operative then that would certainly be looked upon in a positive way.'

Stop now! Say no more, Melanie, Cornish thought.

The solicitor spoke again to his client. For a moment, she remained silent, wiping tears from her cheeks with her fingers. She then turned to him and spoke for some time.

Ashraf Mohammed listened intently as she talked. When she eventually fell silent he reached for a glass of water and took a long gulp.

Hugo Constantine glanced at Melanie and raised his eyebrows.

Come on! What do you know? Melanie thought, trying to remain calm.

Mr Mohammed raised his hand to his mouth and coughed gently to clear his throat.

Melanie was right, she does know something, Cornish mused.

Mr Mohammed then spoke:

'My client informs me that now the two men are dead she feels that she is able to speak more freely about the murders.'

I knew she was involved! Melanie thought, and said:

'So she admits she is involved in this case and has knowingly held back what could be vital information ?' Melanie asked.

'…That depends on how you view, *involved*,' the solicitor replied.

'Does your client realise that it is an offence to pervert the course of justice in the UK?'

Mohammed nodded. 'Unequivocally, Miss Underwood. My client has remained silent because she was under the threat of *death*. Not an unreasonable action in the circumstances, I'm sure you'll agree?'

Melanie was about to respond when the solicitor raised his hand and said:

'And—you must remember,' he stressed, 'that these men were not Muslims—they were dangerous, radical extremists. The kind that tarnish the good name of the millions of normal, peaceful Muslims living in the world today.'

Melanie decided not to reply. Her mind had flashed back to the warehouse rooftop and the feeling of the cold blade pressing into her neck. Instead she glanced at her notes for a moment to compose herself…. Looking up she asked:

'I want to understand the relationship between your client and the two dead jihadis?' Her tone was authoritative.

The solicitor then talked to his client for some time.

Eventually he turned to regard Melanie again and said:

'In February of this year, my client was approached by the two of them. They informed her that it was necessary for them to carry out Allah's wishes, but they gave her no details of their intentions. They insisted that she gave them the access codes to the building and the Russian's apartment. They warned her of the dire consequences if she didn't keep silent about it.'

Melanie looked at Miss Halabi. 'Can you ask your client where she was at two o'clock in the morning, on the Monday of the murders?'

The eventual response to the question was that she was in bed, asleep.

Melanie continued her questioning:

'We have video evidence of a woman, wearing a burka, visiting the apartment at that time with the two jihadis.' Melanie turned her laptop to face them and played the video at the moment when the three suspects entered the main door to the building.

'Is the woman in the video your client Mr Mohammed?'

Another discussion pursued and eventually the solicitor answered:

'My client swears that she is not the woman in the video.'

Melanie responded with another question:

'Does she *know* who the woman in the video is?'

The solicitor hesitated and coughed nervously before replying.

'…She believes the woman is Sami Karam's sister.'

Melanie frowned, taken aback by the answer. 'Surely you don't mean—Jamal Karam?'

'No—Sami Karam had four sisters.'

'But… I understood that only Sami and Jamal survived the conflict in Syria!'

Mr Mohammed shook his head. 'No, Miss Underwood, that's not true. The eldest sister, Fatima, also survived Assad's brutal onslaughts.'

'So where is Fatima Karam now?'

The solicitor removed his glasses and wiped them with a tissue from his pocket.

'Please answer the question.'

'…My client doesn't know where she is.'

'…So your client is suggesting that Jamal Karam was decapitated by her *own* sister?'

The interpreter interjected:

'Jamal's sister was a very devout Muslim. Sadly, like her brother Sami, it appears that she was radicalised too.'

'Really?' was Melanie's response. 'Personally, I don't believe Sami was radicalised. They *failed* to turn him into a monster,' she stressed, with a hint of affection in her voice.

The solicitor glared at Hugo Constantine and snarled:

'If I want your input I will ask for it! Is that clear?'

Melanie tensed, clearly irritated by the solicitor's brusque comment and asked him:

'So, did Fatima Karam also decapitate Maksim Mikhailov?'

The solicitor huffed, defiantly. '…My client has no knowledge of the events that took place in the apartment during the early hours, because *she* wasn't there, Miss Underwood. She is only aware of what she witnessed when she arrived at the apartment at nine-thirty on that dreadful Monday morning.'

You're getting annoyed now, girl—time to stop! Melanie nodded and checked her watch. '…I believe we've achieved as much as we possibly can today. For the record, I would like to thank Miss Halabi for her valuable contribution to this enquiry. I realise it must have been a very difficult time for her.' Melanie then closed the lid of her laptop. 'The time now is four-fifty pm and this interview is terminated.' Melanie leaned over and switched off the recorder. 'Thank you all for attending today,' she concluded, before standing up and stealing a furtive glance at Cornish.

Alan Cornish nodded his approval:

Well done my love. Another piece fits into the jigsaw. You were bloody impressive. All we need to do now is find the woman in the burka. The proverbial needle in a haystack!

Melanie and Cornish escorted their visitors to the main entrance and said their goodbyes. Ashraf Mohammed and Miss Halabi walked out together onto the forecourt, leaving Hugo Constantine alone. He turned to Melanie and in a quiet voice he said:

'Miss Underwood, I think you should be aware that when you asked about Fatima Karam's whereabouts and Mr Mohammed said that his client didn't know where she was… Well, off the record, Miss Underwood—although I genuinely believe Miss Halabi doesn't know Fatima Karam's whereabouts, she did mention that the *Imam* had *recently* been in conversation with her.'

'You mean in conversation with Fatima Karam?'

'Yes, precisely, but Mr Mohammed either chose, or forgot to mention that fact in the interview.'

Melanie glanced in surprise at Cornish and said:

'Now *that* is very interesting!'

Melanie then offered her hand to the interpreter. 'Thank you Mr Constantine, thank you *very* much,' she said, 'you've been a great help.'

Chapter 31

LET SLEEPING DOGS LIE

Metropolitan Police Headquarters, Victoria Embankment.

Chief Superintendent Montgomery stood up and smiled when Neil Bartholomew from MI6 walked into his office. 'Good morning Neil,' he said brightly, holding out his hand. The tall man with the gold-rimmed glasses approached and reached over the large desk to shake his hand:

'And a very good morning to you, Chief Superintendent,' he replied, equally brightly.

Montgomery gestured to him to take a seat in front of his desk and Bartholomew duly settled on the conference chair.

'Would you like tea or coffee, Neil?' Montgomery asked.

'That depends, Chief Superintendent.'

Montgomery tilted his head in a questioning way. 'On what?'

'Is it out of a machine?'

'Normally, yes, but my secretary makes extremely good tea and coffee when requested.'

'Excellent, then I'll have an extremely good black coffee, if you please, made by your secretary,' Bartholomew replied.

'Yes,' was Montgomery's terse reply as he walked out of the office… On his return he said, 'the coffee won't be long. Sally's grinding the *one-hundred-percent* Arabica beans as we speak.'

Bartholomew allowed himself a wry smile, missed by Montgomery as he returned to his seat behind the desk.

'So—what have you got to report, Chief Superintendent?'

Montgomery settled himself and brushed a hair off the sleeve of uniform… 'I had a meeting with Alan Cornish yesterday and it appears that he's now taking *two* separate lines of enquiry, as he believes the murders of the Russian and his girlfriend were actually two separate incidents.'

Bartholomew tapped his bottom lip with his index finger. 'Why does he believe that?'

'He believes that the Russian was shot by a professional assassin on the Sunday evening and that the beheadings took place later, in the early hours of Monday morning, by the two jihadis and a woman accomplice, wearing a burka.'

Bartholomew stroked his cheek. 'Tell me more about this— professional assassin, Chief Superintendent?'

'There is little to tell, I'm afraid, Neil. Cornish is actually no closer to identifying him.'

'So how does Cornish know about the assassin?'

'Apparently he disguised himself as a local delivery man carrying a parcel and got access to the apartment that way. He then vanished into the night.'

'Like a true professional!'

At that moment Montgomery's secretary tapped on the door and walked in with two coffee mugs and a selection of biscuits on a tray.

'Leave then on the desk, Sally,' Montgomery said, leaning over to see what biscuits they were.

'Rich Tea and shortbreads, sir,' she replied, glancing at the well dressed man sitting in front of the desk.

'Coffee smells good,' Bartholomew said with a smile.

The secretary smiled back and walked out of the office.

'…I don't know about you, Chief Superintendent, but I'm not happy spending government money funding Cornish anymore. At least not for two separate lines of enquiry. I think we should get Probe to wrap the case up asap and drop the assassin thing all together—right now. We'll just have to accept the fact that the young Russian was killed—probably by a Russian assassin—but there is clearly not enough evidence to prove it. The important thing is that the top-secret Russian information didn't get into the wrong hands. It's now in the *safe* hands of MI6.' The tall man leaned forward and picked up a coffee and a biscuit from the desk. 'The assassination details will not be made public of course.'

Deep in thought, Montgomery bit into a shortbread. 'Of course not. That would just complicate things. The public doesn't need to be confused with *irrelevant* details. The original statement has been verified by Cornish's findings anyway. If he wants to pursue the woman involved, then that's up to him. I'm prepared to fund him for one more week on the basis that he terminates his line of enquiry looking for the Russian's killer.' Montgomery chuckled. 'It certainly won't do any harm.'

'Quite honestly, Chief Superintendent, I don't give a fuck who killed the woman. Domestic violence is not my domain. My interests are based purely on matters that threaten national security.' Bartholomew then got to his feet and said:

'One more week and then wrap it up... This coffee is excellent by the way.'

Montgomery smiled, knowing the machine it came from. 'Do you want me to call in the Russian Ambassador, Neil?'

'No, I don't think so—not under the circumstances. We have absolutely no proof of Russia's involvement in any of this. To call him in would be futile and probably highly embarrassing for us. Believe me, the Russians are experts at denial!... Let sleeping dogs lie, Chief Superintendent...Wouldn't you agree?'

Montgomery grinned, smugly. 'Absolutely, Neil—let sleeping dogs lie,' he said, as they shook hands across the desk.

*

Alan Cornish put the phone down after the short conversation with Chief Superintendent Montgomery and stormed out of his office towards the coffee machine.

Melanie noticed him from her desk and realised there was something wrong. She walked over to meet him and asked:

'What's wrong, love?'

'I've just had a conversation with that prat of a chief superintendent.'

'And?'

'He has instructed us to immediately terminate the enquiry into the Russian's death. He said, as we have no leads to work on the costly effort was futile and unproductive.'

'What!'

'And condescendingly, he's given us one more week to find the girl in the burka. After that the funding stops.'

'But he's not the policy maker is he? He's just a puppet.' Melanie pointed out.

'Yeah, you're right. He's been got at by Bartholomew and that man has his own agenda, which I'm still trying to get my head around.'

'…So what are you going to do?' Melanie asked.

Cornish pursed his lips and said defiantly:

'…Fuck the lot of 'em. Let's call a meeting!'

'I knew you'd say that,' Melanie replied, and gave Cornish a supportive hug.

'We're going to find Fatima Karam and we're going to find the assassin; with, or without, the help of the Metropolitan Police or MI6.'

'*Yeah!*' she replied.

'Melanie, get the team together and let's meet in my office in half an hour. I'm going to give Christopher Copeland a quick call to see if he's found something for us to bite on.'

'Yes boss!' Melanie replied, and walked away with a purposeful stride.

Chapter 32

FUNDING OR NO FUNDING

Melanie had duly spoken to Zeezee, Tom Weiss and Zac Monde and one-by-one they gathered in Cornish's office with a few minutes to spare before the start of the meeting. There was an air of expectation in the room and Cornish looked relaxed sitting on the edge of his desk. He glanced at Melanie and asked:

'Are we all here?'

'Yes, we are,' she replied.

'Good—let's make a start then.' Cornish stood and faced his audience. 'If you don't already know, the Met has requested that we cease investigating the murder of the Russian, Maksim Mikhailov, immediately. We have also been given just one more week to find the burka woman. So let's analyse those instructions for a moment. The Russian was shot in the head and decapitated, but the Met are now not interested in finding his killer; even though at the last meeting, the man from MI6 was happy to double our rate! And then there's his girlfriend's killers. If the woman in the burka is not found within a week, the Met will close the case anyway, with no further comment in the case file about her!'

Tom Weiss asked:

'So what the fuck is going on Boss? Why have they changed their minds again?'

'To be honest Tom, I don't know—but it's obvious that MI6 is running the show...I must stress, guys, that these are the instructions from our client. What *we* choose to do, of course, is up to us. Personally, I have no intention of terminating the enquiry into the death of the Russian, or his girlfriend and we will continue, as a team, to investigate the murders until we get a result.'

The team members smiled and nodded their approval. Tom Weiss fist-pumped the air!

Cornish continued:

'At this moment in time we have just two leads to follow up. Our investigations have led us to believe that the woman wearing the burka is actually Jamal Karam's radicalised elder sister, Fatima Karam, whom we initially believed to be dead. Team—we need to find her, and we need to find her fast! We also now know, thanks to Copeland and Associates, that the knockout dart used on Jamal Karam was manufactured in

Prague and I intend to investigate that enigma further too, funding or no funding from the Met!'

Melanie then spoke:

'We believe that Fatima Karam is still in London and I have arranged to see the Imam at the mosque tomorrow after midday prayers, because we know he's been in conversation with her recently. Hopefully, if he knows her whereabouts, he will co-operate with us.'

Cornish interjected:

'But remember, this woman is highly dangerous. None of us are to approach her without the appropriate backup in place. Is that quite clear?' he asked, briefly glancing at Melanie.

Chapter 33

THE PARK BENCH

Salat al-zuhr, midday prayers, had finished and the mosque was emptying. Melanie was standing outside the main entrance knowing the next hour or so would be crucial if they were to find Fatima Karam. Even though the result of their first meeting was a disaster, she hoped that the diminutive figure with the limp would still co-operate with her; but if she was honest with herself, her expectations were low.

There he is, she thought, as the Imam walked out into the bright sunshine. Melanie raised the scarf over her head and approached him with a smile.

'Hello young lady,' he said.

'Hello,' she replied, 'thank you for agreeing to see me again.'

'Is it my turn to buy the tea?' he asked.

Melanie relaxed and said:

'Don't worry, I'll claim it on my expenses, Imam.'

The old man laughed and they walked off together in the direction of the cafe.

Inside, they settled at the same table as their previous visit, overlooking the mosque, and they were served by the same waitress; Melanie remembered her.

'Are you trying to find someone else?' the Imam asked.

'Yes, I am.'

'The last person that I helped you to find is now dead.'

Melanie lowered her head. 'Yes, I know. His death was a tragedy.'

'Don't blame yourself, young lady. Sami Karam would have died with or without your involvement.'

Melanie looked up, surprised by the Imam's conciliatory comment.

'You cannot *negotiate* with radical extremists, Miss Underwood.'

'Those men were monsters, Imam! I watched them shoot Sami in the head and then throw him off the roof of the warehouse because he would not carry out their wishes!'

'And the boy survived! They failed to kill him. In the end I believe the young man welcomed death.'

'Yes, I believe that too,' Melanie replied, 'he wanted to die,' she said, wiping a tear from her cheek.

'Did you get to know him, Miss Underwood?'

'A little,—not well—but enough to know he wasn't a jihadi.'

The Imam laughed. 'He was a sad, misguided boy who fell into the wrong hands and I must accept some of the responsibility for that. I knew what was happening and I chose to ignore the fact that he was being radicalised.'

'Like his sister, Fatima,' Melanie replied.

The Imam looked shocked. 'You know Fatima?' he asked.

Melanie waited while the waitress placed a coffee and a tea on the table, then she responded:

'We now believe it was Fatima that visited the Russian's apartment, with two male accomplices early Monday morning, and there she helped to decapitate her own sister. We *know* that she had been radicalised, Imam.'

'How do you know this, Miss Underwood?'

'We recently interviewed the dead Russian's cleaning lady, Miss Halabi, and she told us. She also told us that you have been in contact with Fatima, Imam. Is that true?'

The Imam sipped his tea and Melanie waited for a response.

'I don't know this Halabi lady, he admitted.'

'But do you admit to knowing Fatima Karam?'

Moments later he asked:

'Will you walk with me, Miss Underwood' he replied.

Melanie frowned. 'Yes, yes of course' she replied. 'Where are you taking me?'

The sun was high in a cloudless, blue canopy and the leafy east London park was alive with people walking their dogs, noisy children playing on the swings and climbing frames and families enjoying picnics on the expanse of grass. It seemed a long way from London, and even the air smelt fresh to Melanie as she walked with the Imam towards a shady park bench.

'May we join you?' the Imam asked a woman, wearing a black hijab, sitting on the far end of the bench.

She replied in Arabic and the Imam settled on the bench. He gestured to Melanie to join him in the middle of the bench.

The Arab woman called out to a young boy playing on the grass in a tone that sounded like a chastisement to Melanie.

'Why have you brought me here, Imam?' Melanie asked.

The Imam smiled. 'Because I want you to meet Fatima Karam, Miss Underwood.'

Melanie immediately tensed. 'What!' Alan's voice sounded in her head:

Remember, this woman is highly dangerous. None of us are to approach her without the appropriate backup protocols in place. Is that quite clear?

'Where is she?' she asked, anxiously. 'because I'm not sure —'

The Imam took hold of Melanie's hand 'There is no need to feel fear,' he said, reassuringly. 'Fatima is sitting next to you,

Miss Underwood, and that's her young son playing on the grass. He will be three next month.'

Melanie glanced at the young woman next to her who smiled back. The shape of her dark eyes and her prominent nose left Melanie in no doubt that this woman was Sami Karam's sister. Melanie wanted to speak but suddenly no words seemed appropriate.

'I think you're looking for the wrong woman,' Miss Underwood, the Imam responded.

'Yes, I think you're right.' Melanie admitted. 'Do you speak English, Miss Karam?'

'Yes, I do,' she replied.

'I was saddened by the death of your brother.'

'Thank you. He was manipulated—by very bad people.'

'Yes, I know.'

'They recognised his devotion to Allah, but they recognised his venerability too, which they exploited.' Fatima struggled to catch her breath for a moment. '…They corrupted him and tried to turn him into a jihadi—but Sami could *never* have been a jihadi,' she stressed, glancing up at the sky.

Melanie watched as tears ran down her cheeks.

Fatima turned to look at Melanie. 'I guess you know that Jamal gave up the faith and became a common *whore*, bringing shame upon our family name?'

Melanie's initial reaction was to contradict her, but she decided that now wasn't the time.

Fatima continued:

'They wanted him to kill his sister for her sins. You see, they needed him to prove to them that he was a *true* jihadi. But in his heart my brother still loved her. Sami simply wasn't capable of killing anyone; no matter how hard that monster tried to groom him.'

'Which monster are you referring to, Fatima?'

'The monster who trained him, in Afghanistan, to decapitate non-believers. Any ideology that actively promotes the taking of human life must *not* be tolerated.'

Melanie offered a weak smile. 'Thankfully that monster was shot dead on the roof of the warehouse.'

Fatima looked confused. 'Oh no! *She* is very much alive and here in London!'

'*She?*' Melanie exclaimed.

Fatima nodded. The Imam turned to face Fatima and asked:

'Why have you not told me about this person?'

'Because I'm frightened of monsters!…I have nightmares about her after listening to Sami's stories of what she did in Afghanistan; she killed my sister. But, she won't stop there; not until she achieves martyrdom. She could kill me and my son too just for talking to you!'

Melanie reached across and held her hand for reassurance. 'She's not going to do that. We'll protect you and your son.'

'Tell Miss Underwood her name, Fatima!' the Imam demanded.

Fatima took a deep breath and exhaled to compose herself. 'You already know her. Her name is, Yara Halabi!'

'Oh my god!' Melanie cried out, clasping her hands around her face.

*

Probes Office's Cambridge later that day

'She's vanished into thin air,' Cornish announced, 'her solicitor, has no idea where she's gone; although I'm not sure I believe him!'

'What did CS Montgomery have to say for himself?' Melanie asked.

'Oh yes—the Chief Superintendent! Now that was an interesting conversation, because you've *really* upset the apple cart now, my love,' Cornish said, rubbing his hands together in delight. 'What was a botched robbery has now turned into an international murder hunt for a suspect that the CIA and MI6 have been trying to identify for the last two years.'

Melanie smirked and bit into her biscuit.

Cornish returned to his captain's chair and started to tap his fingertips together.

'What are you thinking?'

'I'm thinking about what worries me,' he replied.

'And what exactly is it that's worrying you?'

'…Why would such a high-profile terrorist, like her, come to *London* and risk blowing her cover? She didn't come here just to kill Jamal Karam for being a naughty girl, that's for sure. There has to be far more to it than that, Melanie and I think we could be in for a rough ride in the near future!'

Melanie's appetite suddenly waned. 'You're suggesting she's planning a terrorist attack, aren't you?'

'Yes, I am!' Pensively, Cornish inhaled, then exhaled, slowly. '…I think we need a large glass of wine down by the side of the river, don't you?'

Melanie forced a smile. 'I think you know the answer to that one,' she replied. '…I wonder what Vera would have made of her—one murderer to another? …I must admit Alan, she's probably the most *audacious* person I've ever met,' Melanie confessed.

Cornish chuckled. 'And we thought Vera was dangerous! It must have been Halabi who decapitated the dead Russian.'

'What—Just for the fun of it?'

'Yeah! Dead Russians are good to practice on.'

A shiver ran down Melanie's spine. 'And to think I ordered that monster not to leave the country! She must have been laughing at me all the while. What a bloody nerve!'

'True, but without you she might never have been identified and I don't think she has any intentions of going anywhere. She's on a *mission*.'

Chapter 34

IT'S ONLY JUST BEGINNING

'Melanie's discovery has changed the rules of engagement,' Cornish explained to his assembled team. 'The race to find Yara Halabi is now *officially* out of our hands, guys. We must hope and pray that our security forces find her before she does some real damage, because we believe that is exactly what she has planned.'

'To do that in this country is not easy.' Tom Weiss stressed. 'She must have a network of people that are somehow staying below the radar. Does the anti-terrorist squad have much on her, Boss?'

Cornish raised his hands. 'They only knew of her existence, but they didn't know her identity until Melanie exposed her. They thought she was still in the mountains of Afghanistan training jihadis to decapitate infidels!'

Tom Weiss replied:

'And Melanie found out simply by talking to Fatima Karam in a London park! That is scary.'

'Yes, but let's not forget, Tom, Fatima Karam is an illegal immigrant. Technically she doesn't exist and if she's not rocking the boat the chances are she could live happily in this country for the rest of her life, under the radar. Saying that, she and her son have now been taken into protective custody for their own safety, until further notice. The big difference is that now Yara Halabi is exposed, she cannot work incognito anymore; she's been forced to go underground.'

'You mean she now has to walk around the city in a burka.'

'Good point, Tom,' Cornish conceded.

'So is our involvement effectively over now?' Melanie asked, with an air of resignation.

'…Officially yes, but in reality, no, it's not over yet, Mel,' Cornish replied. 'Montgomery has informed me that none of this is being released to the press in the near future. The authorities are still working hard trying to agree a strategy. Don't expect to see Yara Halabi's name all over the tabloids tomorrow. Panic is the last thing they want, so it's crucial that we respect that silence too. I still want you, Tom, to keep your ears to the ground in the city regarding this Yara Halabi woman without kicking up any dust at all. Do what you do best, okay?'

'Sure thing, Boss, if that's what you want,' Weiss replied, enthusiastically.

Cornish continued:

'So now we know who she is, let's get as much information to hand as possible about her skill sets, because I think she will play to her strengths, *whatever* they are. We already know she's an expert at decapitation but that's all we really know about her.'

'Fancy having that on your CV!' jibed Tom Weiss. 'That would give HR a few issues!'

Cornish chuckled and continued:

'Clearly, she's audacious, radical, probably highly intelligent and a fearless *monster!*... Zeezee, see what you can dig up about her on the—dark—onion thing that you use.'

Zeezee laughed. 'You mean the *Dark Web*,' he replied, politely.

'Yeah, that's it!' Cornish agreed. 'It just might give us a clue as to what she's planning.' Cornish stopped to take a sip of water. 'Amongst all of this excitement it could be easy to forget that I still want to stay focussed on finding our assassin too. Zeezee has come up with some more information that might be critical to our enquiries... So, no, it's not over, team. In fact, I think it's only just beginning, and once again, we're on our own.'

*

Melanie's Apartment

Melanie took a long shower and then walked naked from the bathroom into the bedroom. Cornish held out a tumbler of iced gin and tonic but quickly changed his mind, as he watched her approach him, and placed the drink down on the bedside table.

'You are so beautiful,' he said, in awe.

'Thank you, now fuck me hard,' she said, seductively, as she pushed him onto the bed and straddled him.

'You strike a hard bargain,' Cornish replied.

'Not nearly as hard as your bargain, darling,' Melanie uttered in pleasure, as Cornish entered her. 'I really needed this today, love.'

'Glad to be of service, ma'am.'

Melanie laughed and then took full control of the next twenty minutes, to the sheer delight of Alan Cornish; who'd convinced himself he was dreaming, every time they made love.

Thirty minutes and three-quarters of a bottle of Hendricks later they were asleep in each others arms; blissfully unaware of the daring, terrorist attack being planned to inflict utter carnage in the heart of London.

Chapter 35

'ALLAHU AKBAR'

Somewhere in east London

The seven men nodded and muttered their approval to the woman standing in front of them as cigarette and fragrant joss stick smoke choked the air in the small, east London flat like a thick, sixties smog.

'Let me make it very clear to each and every one of you. I *expect* total obedience. My rules are strict—nobody disobeys me! Is that clear?' Yara Halabi demanded in Arabic 'We will *never* use mobile phones to communicate. We will communicate only by word-of-mouth and the written word, and the written word will be Arabic, *never* English.'

The seven men nodded their approval.

'I expect every one of you to be prepared to die for the cause. Do not be afraid of becoming a martyr, there is no pain; consider it an honour to go to Jannah. We will strike at the very

191

heart of the evil that has killed so many of us around the world. But our strike will be devastating, unexpected and shocking. It will rock the very foundations that this country is build on, tearing apart this vile establishment and leading the way to an Islamic Republic that will soon wrap its wings around the world. *Allahu Akbar!'*

'Allahu Akbar,' was the frenzied response to Yara Halabi's stirring words.

'Our attack will take the UK and the world by complete surprise. In Afghanistan and the Middle East our enemies drones kill our soldiers and religious leaders every day; but now, we have the chance to turn the tide. They will not expect a drone attack of this nature. It will be *our* drones that will be killing *our* enemies…Soldiers of Islam—this is my master plan.' Yara Halabi gazed at the expectant faces in front of her for a brief moment and then said:

'In June of every year, in London, Trooping the Colour celebrates the official birthday of this country's monarch. It is a spectacle, watched the world over. But soon the world will watch in horror, as this country's monarch is slaughtered in front of their eyes; along with over 1400 parading soldiers, 200 horses and 400 musicians. All of this will be achieved with just twenty drones. Disbelieving eyes will witness the carnage that will turn their blood ice-cold and they will bow down in front of us, chanting *Allahu Akbar!'*

'Allahu Akbar!'

'But let us not be complacent. To achieve our goal will not be an easy task. In this country, walls have ears and we must work like the silent spirits that leave no footprints in the desert sand. Talk to nobody about our plans other than those around you in this room. If you do talk, I will cut your tongue out and then I will cut off your head, just like I did to the whore, Jamal Karam, and her Russian pimp; to make *doubly* sure that you don't do it again.' Yara Halabi smiled for the first time.

A few nervous laughs faded away very quickly as cigarettes were quickly lit with lighters held in hands that trembled with trepidation and the adrenalin that was surging through their veins like hot lava.

'Rejoice in the future my brave soldiers, because our task is the will of Allah and we will not fail. *Allahu Akbar!'*

'Allahu Akbar!'

Chapter 36

WHAT'S ALL THIS ABOUT

Probe's Offices

'Tell us what you've found out about Yara Halabi, Zeezee?' Cornish asked, with obvious enthusiasm.

Zeezee walked to the centre of the conference room and faced his colleagues. He coughed gently to clear his throat and then spoke:

'I have spent the last two days gathering information about Yara Halabi. Obviously, you're not going to find her picture on the front of Time Magazine, but we know what she looks like as she had the audacity to visit our offices on two occasions!' Zeezee flashed up a recent photo of the woman on the large screen behind him, showing her in a group of rifle wielding terrorists. 'According to the CIA, this was taken somewhere in Afghanistan within the last two months. As you can see it's impossible to identify anyone in the picture, but I'm reliably informed that it is her. She has been instrumental in training jihadis for over two years, somewhere in the Hindu Kush Mountains. She is an expert in armed combat, military drones and explosives. The CIA believes that Iran has been secretly funding her operation to the tune of four-hundred-thousand-pounds, plus military hardware and arms.'

'Where is she from?' Melanie asked.

'As far as we know she's originally from the Lebanon, Melanie, but she moved to Iraq to join the fighting. Yara Halabi is her nom de guerre. There is still some dispute about her real name and she has no known siblings. She got married to a jihadi in Iraq, but he was killed by British Special Forces four years ago. She survived a Russian rocket attack three years ago in Syria and after that she headed off to the mountains of Afghanistan. We believe she arrived in the UK very recently using a false passport, and remember, non of the intelligence services knew who she was until Melanie identified her.'

Tom Weiss rubbed his chin and said:

'So clearly this woman has a grudge against the UK and Russia, which might explain why she decapitated the dead Russian. One thing's for sure though, she's not here for a holiday!'

'That's true, Tom,' Cornish agreed. 'She's definitely here to cause trouble. She's an expert in armed combat, explosives and —what else, Zeezee?'

'Iranian military drones, Alan.'

'Not something you'd find on Amazon then?'

'But without the help of the security forces and the Met, it's going to be almost impossible for us to track her down.' Tom Weiss suggested.

Cornish stood up. 'Yes, you're right, Tom, but someone knows where she is, because something like this takes a lot of organising. She needs help and somewhere to stay. Do we know where she was staying while she was the *harmless* cleaner for the Russian?'

Melanie responded:

'Yes, we have an address where she was staying before she went to ground.'

'Okay, Tom, will you check out the area around there. Find out who she's been hanging out with?'

'Yeah sure,' replied Weiss.

'Melanie, do you think it's worth talking to the Imam again?' Cornish asked.

'It's worth a try, Alan. I don't think we've got anything to lose by it.'

'Okay go and see him. Zeezee, let's get a list of the upcoming events in the city for, say the next two months, that she might consider a target? Can you also get me the specs for the Iranian drones that she knows so much about?'

Zeezee smiled, having already anticipated the question. 'You mean the Shahed 129, their biggest UCAV.'

'UCAV?' Cornish repeated.

'Unmanned combat aerial vehicle,' Zeezee, explained.

'No, something much smaller than that; something more portable and commercial, not military.'

'Like what?'

'To be honest, I don't know,' Cornish replied. 'I'm just thinking out loud. What about commercial drones that can carry a heavy payload?'

'Ah! Now we need to call in the expert.'

'Who's that?' Cornish asked.

'Our very own, Zac Monde; he's a drone enthusiast.'

'Let's get him in, Cornish enthused, picking up the phone.'

Moments later the blonde haired, blue-eyed comms expert, Zac Monde, walked into the office.

'Zac, come and join us and take a seat,' Cornish said, eagerly. 'I understand that you're a bit of a drone enthusiast?'

'Yeah, I have a couple,' Zac replied, 'why's that?'

Cornish interlocked his fingers, pensively, and then asked:

'If I wanted to buy a commercial drone, that was capable of carrying a workload, what kind of weight could I expect to carry?'

Zac pondered on the question as he settled on a chair next to Melanie. He then answered:

'…There are a number of drones on the market and their pay loads can vary from one kilo to ten kilos, but they're not cheap.'

Cornish nodded. 'That's twenty-two pounds in old money,' he said, 'well over a stone!'

'If you say so,' Zac responded. 'What's all this about?'

'…If someone wanted to use a commercial drone to carry some kind of weapon then I guess that would be possible, wouldn't it?'

Zac Monde pondered the question. '…Well, I guess so, Alan. I've never really thought about it to be honest.'

'I wonder if Yara Halabi has thought about it?' Cornish asked, in an open question to the group.

'What kind of weapon are you thinking about, Alan?' Tom Weiss asked.

'…I'm thinking about some kind of—*chemical* weapon,' Cornish replied.

'What, like—nerve gas?'

Cornish shrugged. 'Well, it's possible, Tom. Nerve gas is not very heavy, is it?'

'Very true, but how many people have access to nerve gas in the UK?'

'I agree, but we're dealing with a terrorist who has connections in Syria, Iran, Iraq and Afghanistan, where the stuff can be bought on a street stall! Illegal drugs are smuggled into the UK every day, so it's not inconceivable that she has found a way to bring it in. But before we all panic, let's just keep in mind that this is Alan Cornish's hypothesis. It is not based on *any* evidence.'

'And do you have a target in mind for this hypothetical attack, Alan?' Melanie asked, tentatively.

'Now, *that* is the million-dollar question, Melanie! If Yara Halabi was planning a nerve-gas attack somewhere in London, in the near future, using drones, what target would she choose? Team, we need to find the answer to this *hypothetical* question, and we need to find it fast,' Cornish stressed.

'Presumably it would be an outdoor target?' Melanie suggested.

Cornish nodded in agreement. 'I think that is a very good hypothesis. So what outdoor events with large gatherings do we have coming up in June and July?'

'Trooping the Colour is always on the second Saturday in June,' Melanie stated.

Cornish began to tap his fingers together and she knew that he was seriously appraising her suggestion.

After a long silence he finally said:

'The ultimate target for a fanatical extremist.'

'Seeking revenge for her husband!' Tom Weiss, stressed.

'Exactly, Tom!'

'Are you going to speak to the authorities, Alan?' Melanie asked.

'With no proof, Melanie, I don't think they'd want to know.'

Chapter 37

GHEE BUTTER

The Asian food store in Hanbury Street, off Brick Lane, in London's East End, supplied a large variety of exotic foodstuffs to the local ethnic community. The shop's facade looked tired and neglected, unlike the bright, rebellious graffiti that adorned much of Hanbury Street's walls. But once inside, the piquant smell of fresh coriander and ground cumin invaded the nostrils. Colourful jars of turmeric, paprika, cayenne pepper and garam masala adorned shelves, like an alchemists laboratory; but on the floor, plain wooden boxes stuffed with leafy yardlong beans, bok choy, okra, bitter melons, plantains and open sacks of chickpeas, lentils and Urad flour reminded the visitor that this was just a shop.

Yara Halabi was wearing a black burka as she walked casually into Hanbury Street. Her relaxed walk concealed her inner excitement that stimulated every nerve in her body. She knew that a part of her dream was about to come true; she knew because failure wasn't something she'd ever contemplated. Moments later, as if in a dream, she arrived outside the store. She stopped and looked around before entering the shop. A nervous looking middle-aged man with a bald head and a thick, black moustache greeted her in Arabic, saying:

'As-salam alaykom.'

She replied:

'Wa Alykom As-salam.'

He gestured to her with his hand to follow him as he turned and walked to the back of the store and up a flight of stairs that quickly made him breathless. Yara Halabi followed behind.

Looking up the stairs, she could see two young children smiling down at her, but as she began to ascend the stairs they quickly ran off giggling with excitement.

'They must not be here. You had my instructions,' she called out to the man, who quickly repeated her commands as he gasped for air. A woman appeared and gathered up the children before herding them down the stairs to a plethora of inquisitive questions about the mysterious visitor.

'And tell her not to come back for an hour!'

The man bellowed Yara Halabi's further instructions down the stairs.

Once they were alone in the sudden silence she asked:

'Has it arrived?'

'Yes,' replied the man, 'it arrived this morning.'

'Good—show me,' she said, removing her burka to reveal a grey hoody, green combat trousers and Nike trainers.

'...It's in here.' The man pushed a door open and walked into darkness. He flicked a wall switch and a florescent strip-light flickered into action, eventually illuminating a room full of boxes and tins stacked untidily on metal racks around the walls.

'It's there,' he said, pointing to a large cardboard box, labelled Ghee Butter, on a small table at the back of the storeroom. 'Is it safe?' he asked, nervously.

Yara Halabi laughed. 'Safe? I certainly hope not,' she replied.

The man tried to smile but only managed a nervous twitch of his eyelid.

With a penknife she opened the box and looked down at the top layer of sixteen, shiny tin lids. 'Get me a tin opener,' she demanded.

The man scurried off and returned with the opener.

Removing the top layer of tins, Yara Halabi exposed another middle layer. Some of the tins were, as she expected, marked with a small, red circle; the sight of which immediately brought a smile to her face. She then carefully proceeded to open one of the marked tins. 'Get me a bowl and a spoon,' she said, and the man quickly obliged.

She removed the lid and gently pushed the spoon into the ghee. Then, using the spoon as a lever, she carefully prised a stainless steel tube out of the tin. 'Get me a cloth,' she said, excitedly.

'What is it?' the man asked, as he approached the table.

'Just get me a cloth,' she replied, rubbing her hands together.

The man returned with a white, muslin cloth and handed it to her. She wiped the steel tube clean and then paused, to take a deep breath, before twisting both ends in opposite directions. The tube became two distinct pieces and very carefully she pulled them apart to expose a neatly fitting, glass vial about ten centimetres long, filled with what looked like an innocuous, clear liquid.

The man's brow furrowed. 'What is it?' he asked again.

'It's part of my dream,' replied Yara Halabi. '…Nobody is to come in here, is that clear?'

'But I have—'

'Nobody! Do you understand? …Is this room lockable?'

'Yes!' he said, pointing to the bunch of keys dangling from his waistband.

'Lock it behind me! I will return within the hour and take the tins away. You have done well, Hassan, and I thank you for your loyalty.'

The man nodded in silent acknowledgement, not really knowing what he'd done.

Yara Halabi carefully resealed the steel tube and placed it in a leather pouch, fastened around her waist. She then walked out of the storeroom and slipped the burka back over her head.

She waited and watched as the man locked the store room before saying her goodbyes.

Moments later, she was walking nonchalantly down Hanbury Street, knowing that she now possessed enough Sarin nerve agent to kill 60,000 people, and a self-satisfied smile quickly melted her stoic features. A smile that was hidden from humanity.

Her dream had just moved a quantum leap closer to fruition.

Chapter 38

QUESTIONS

'What have we got, Zeezee?' Cornish asked.

Zeezee rubbed his shaven head and smiled. 'I think I've found something of interest,' he replied.

'I knew you would,' Cornish said, confidently, as he slipped into his captain's chair. 'What have you found then?'

'I've been talking to Interpol about the assassination of the Russian and the use of the thiopental dart.'

Cornish raised his eyebrows in anticipation.

'Interpol has dozens of unsolved murders on the books in Europe, but interestingly, three murder victims were found with thiopental in their blood and all three victims were assassinated with a single shot to the head; one in Holland, one in France and the other in Germany.'

'A pattern—or coincidence?' Cornish asked.

'Thiopental is manufactured in a number of countries, including the Czech Republic, which is where the dart was manufactured, remember?'

'Yeah!'

Zeezee continued:

'Interpol believes that a guy by the name of Tomas Soukal, from the Czech Republic, might be the man we're interested in. He is being watched by Interpol but they have no evidence, as yet, to pull him in. He's clever, he speaks a number of languages and uses a number of different identities and disguises. Interpol say that he travelled to the French coast by car, a few days before the murders. He then, somehow, went to ground for a few days and then turned up again driving back across France to Hamburg, in Germany, where he stayed for a few more days before returning to Prague. Why would he do that? Was he returning from the UK?'

'But there's no record of him being in the UK, is there?'

Zeezee shook his head. 'No, nothing; but—we did a search on cars coming to the UK by ferry. Cars like his S-class Merc; thankfully they're not that common. We found a visitor from Antwerp in Belgium. A young man by the name of Lucas Janssens who, coincidentally, arrived in Dover just before the murders and left just after the murders—and guess what?'

'He had a false passport and false plates.'

'Yeah, precisely.'

'Olly Mathias, that's impressive investigative work! I think you've just found our assassin!'

'You don't call me that very often!' Zeezee replied.

Cornish tapped his fingers together in silence for a while and then asked:

'If I wanted to hire him, how would I go about it?'

Zeezee stroked his beard, pensively. 'You'd need contacts in the criminal underworld, Alan, and you'd be vetted too. As a private investigator, I'd suggest *your* chances of hiring an assassin were pretty slim.'

'I wasn't thinking of me. I was thinking more like—Tom!'

'Tom?'

'Yeah! You know the plot: ex-bent copper from New York looking for the whistle-blower, with Italian blood, who claimed witness immunity from prosecution, which, by the way, cost Tom his job and his pension at the NYPD, and then moved to Italy under a new identity and all paid for by the witness protection programme.'

'Oh yeah—that plot!' Zeezee replied, shaking his head incredulously.

'Just thinking out loud,' Cornish added.

'Have you mentioned this to Tom yet?'

'No, not yet, I'm still working on it.'

'So let me get this straight. Tom Weiss is going to somehow find and approach this assassin, Tomas Soukal, under the pretext of paying him for a contract to kill this whistle-blower chap from America, with Italian ancestry, who now lives in Italy under a new identity?'

'Yeah, something like that.'

'Does he have a name, this whistle-blower?'

Cornish's eyes glanced around the room looking for the answer, 'Gino,' he replied.

'And what happens *after* Tom finds the assassin?' Zeezee asked.

'Ah!—Now *that* bit is still *very* embryonic; but I'm working on it,' Cornish stressed.

'So far, judging by his car, our assassin has made a good living killing people and, at the same time, successfully eluding Interpol. So I would suggest, Alan, that it's not going to be *easy* to track him down and lock him up!'

Cornish smiled. 'To be honest, Zeezee, I'm not really interested in locking him up.'

Zeezee frowned. '…So why are you bothering to chase him at all?'

'…Because I have some questions that I need answers to.'

'Questions? What sort of questions?'

'…Questions, that if answered *truthfully*, will make sense of this whole bloody enigma. Can you have a look on that onion thing of yours to see if his name comes up?'

'You mean the Dark Web.'

'Yeah!' said Cornish, '…come on, it's your turn to make the coffee.'

'You are a little tease sometimes, Alan.'

'I know,' Cornish replied, and strode out of the office.

Zeezee shook his head and followed. '…Actually it's *your* turn to make the coffee!' he called out.

Cornish turned and said:

'You know what, Zeezee, the more I think about it, the more I realise how desperately unlucky our assassin was. He wasn't expecting Yara Halabi to visit the apartment just hours after he'd done his bit! He probably left the gun in the girl's hand to make it look like she'd murdered the Russian and then Halabi and her henchmen turned up, took the gun with them and spoilt everything for him—and his *client*!'

'Whoever that might be,' replied Zeezee.

Cornish smiled to himself, knowingly, and said:

'Whoever, indeed!'

Chapter 39

A FAVOUR REPAID

As promised, Yara Halabi retuned to Hassan's shop within the hour and took away all of the tins of ghee butter marked with a red dot. The tins were placed in a plastic box and carried out to an awaiting Land Rover Vogue, parked outside the shop by a man Hassan did not recognise.

He watched them as they drove away and then he walked back into his shop, deep in thought, wondering what on earth it was all about? Why would anyone hide something in ghee butter? It wasn't drugs—at least he didn't think so. But it must have been something illegal, and she did say it wasn't safe! So what was it?

Her stern words were still ringing his ears:

Do not mention this to anyone. If you do, you and your family will regret it. Do you understand?

She'd frightened him with her aggressive attitude and he began to worry about what he'd done. But at least now he'd repaid the favour to the elder, who'd helped him raise the finances needed to set up his business.

*

Melanie walked towards the now familiar, east London park bench and she smiled when she saw the Imam already there. He noticed her and returned the smile as she approached.

'Not such a nice day today is it?' he said, as Melanie joined him on the bench.

'Not a bit like our last visit,' Melanie replied, and then they sat together in awkward silence for a few moments.

'…So… what is it this time, Miss Underwood?' the Imam asked.

Melanie seemed to be searching for the right words as she rubbed her brow. '…Imam, we believe that there is a very high chance of a *major* terrorist attack in London in the near future.'

The Imam lowered his head. ' You mean an *Islamic* terrorist attack, don't you?'

'Yes, I do.'

'What do you mean by *major,* young lady?'

Melanie took a deep breath to compose herself. 'We believe that this attack will be a *co-ordinated* effort and it will target a mass gathering of people, to kill as many of them as possible; innocent men, women and children.'

The Imam pensively raised his hands to his mouth. 'This is not something I wanted to hear, Miss Underwood.'

'I wish it wasn't true, but we believe it is and we cannot ignore it.'

'Something like this could irrevocably damage the Muslim community in this country and around the world. This is not what peaceful Muslims want at all. We want to live in peace and harmony.—What is it you want of me, Miss Underwood?'

'I want you to tell me if you hear of anything that might help us to stop this attack happening. Anything, Imam! A rumour, a whisper, a stranger in the area acting suspiciously; anything—no matter how irrelevant it might appear to be at the time.'

'These are dark times,' the Imam replied, ruefully.

'Will you help us?'

The Imam nodded his head and forced a smile. 'I cannot promise you anything, Miss Underwood,' he replied, 'other than my word that I will tell you if I suspect someone or something. These people do not mix with the community at large because they are not wanted around here. They are trouble and they will affect our lives in a very detrimental way. They are extremists and they are not welcome in our community.'

Melanie smiled. 'That's all I can ask of you… Let's just pray that you do hear something and that we stop them committing this atrocity.'

The Imam slumped forward. '…Suddenly I feel the weight of the world pressing down upon my shoulders,' he said.

'We want to take some of that weight off your shoulders, Imam,' she replied. 'I hope that Fatima Karam can rejoin your community very soon, but until we find Yara Halabi, she and her son are not safe; along with a lot of other innocent people!'

'There are evil ones out there who believe that Islam can be forced upon the non-believers by pointing a gun at them. This is not what Islam is about. Islam is a way of life, not just a religion, Miss Underwood, but it should be a choice, not a *demand* under fear of death to be a Muslim. Recent years have seen a new, hard face to Islam. It has become impregnated with intolerance and cruelty. We must not allow these people to corrupt our way of life with their dangerous and extremist views. Islam will not survive if it cannot show tolerance and forgiveness in a modern world. It must once again put a high value on *all* human life and learn to live in peace once again; if not, then I fear the worst, because the young will turn and walk away from Islam. They deserve a better life than one of living in constant fear, in bombed-out communities, where families have been devastated or torn apart by war. It breaks my heart to see once thriving communities now living in desolate piles of rubble with little or no hope for the future.'

'You are a good man, Imam. You care about *people*,' Melanie replied, 'and I *share* your hopes for the future. We must not let them win, because life is too precious.'

'Yes, it is, Miss Underwood,' the Imam replied, and then got to his feet. 'I will leave you now and you have my word—I promise to be most vigilant.'

'Thank you, that's all I can ask of you,' she said, and shook his hand, warmly.

The Imam walked away and Melanie noticed that his limp seemed more pronounced.

The weight of the world, pressing down upon his shoulders, she thought.

The man listening to them from a discreet distance stubbed out his cigarette on the grass and followed the Imam as he walked towards the park gates.

As Melanie was making an update call to Cornish, people started screaming and running in all directions. 'Something's just happened, Alan. I'll call you back,' she said, and hurried towards the disturbance. As she neared she could see a man leaning over a person lying on the floor.

'He's been stabbed!' the man called out, 'someone call an ambulance.'

Melanie's heart stopped when she saw that it was the Imam lying motionless on the path. His white-cotton top was soaked in blood and blood was dripping from the side of his mouth. Melanie noticed his hand was trembling. *He's still alive!*

She crouched down close to the Imam and their eyes met.

'Hold on, please—we've called for help and it's on its way,' she said, reassuringly.

The Imam grimaced and coughed, splattering blood onto the path. In a pained, soft voice he uttered:

'Miss Underwood, please don't let them win.' He coughed again and blood filled his throat.

'Hold on Imam,' she said, grasping his pallid hand. 'Please —hold on,' she pleaded. The sound of approaching sirens broke the silence as the old man's trembling hand became still.

Melanie sobbed as she watched the ambulance pull away from the gathered crowd and tears ran down her face as she answered a call from Alan Cornish. She quickly walked off to find a quiet spot saying:

'Yes, no, don't worry, I'm okay,' she stressed before taking a deep breath. '…It's the Imam, Alan, he's been stabbed to death in broad daylight, for talking to me on a park bench for twenty minutes.

Cornish asked if she'd seen the culprit, but Melanie replied that she'd seen nothing.

The gathering crowd was being pushed backwards as more police arrived to quickly cordon off the murder scene with tape. Blue flashing lights and sirens seemed to be everywhere.

'I didn't suspect for one moment that we were being watched,' she said, and began to sob. '…He was a good man, Alan.'

'But his killers must have considered him a real *threat!*' Cornish replied.

'… Why? Can you tell me what the *fuck* these murderers are trying to achieve by killing someone like him?' Melanie's hands shook uncontrollably as she fought to control her emotions. '…His dying words to me were: *"Don't let them win!"* I think we owe him his dying wish, don't you?' she declared, defiantly.

*

Yara Halabi entered Hassan's shop in Hanbury Street wearing the burka that she wore everywhere in public. It was only when she spoke her hello's that the shop owner recognised her and visibly tensed.

'There is one more delivery for me that should arrive here within the next few days, Hassan,' she said.

'Another one?' he replied, with a frown.

'Yes, it will be a large box and when it arrives you must call me immediately—but you must not open it—is that clear?'

'Yes, of course,' he replied. 'May I ask what it is?'

'It is best if you do not know,' Yara Halabi replied.

'Is it dangerous?'

'Many things we do in the name of Allah are dangerous, Hassan. Martyrs offer their lives to God. Never forget that!' She then said her goodbyes and walked out of the shop.

Hassan watched through the shop window as she headed off towards Brick Lane and his stomach began to tighten. He took out a handkerchief and dabbed the beads of perspiration that had appeared on his brow.

Moments later, an old friend entered the shop to inform him of the death of the Imam.

Hassan took the news badly and he struggled to keep his balance. He leaned against the banister at the side of the stairs in an endeavour to steady himself. '…This is terrible! Terrible!' He wiped away tears with his handkerchief that were beginning to blur his vision and he walked, unsteadily, towards the shop entrance. He took the bunch of keys hanging from his belt and quickly selecting the right one, locked the door.

'I am so sorry to bring you such devastating news, Hassan.'

He turned to his friend and asked:

'Do you know how my brother died?'

'…Yes, Hassan,' his friend answered, tentatively.

'Was it a heart attack?'

'... No,... it wasn't. I'm so sorry to have to tell you this, but he was stabbed in the back, as he was leaving the park near the mosque.'

For a brief moment Hassan stood as still as a statue, trying to come to terms with his friends words. '...Stabbed in the back?No!' he cried out, defiantly. 'No! No! No! Do not tell me that my brother was *murdered!* It cannot be true—by brother was an *Imam*—a man of *God*!' he shrieked and began to waver unsteadily before finally collapsing onto the floor.

Chapter 40

THE COMMISSIONER!

Metropolitan Police Headquarters, Victoria Embankment, May 15

'Come in Alan and take a seat.'

'Thank you Chief Superintendent,' Cornish replied as he settled on the conference chair strategically placed in front of Montgomery's desk. He watched Montgomery as he settled on his chair behind his desk. He seemed nervous to Cornish as he adjusted his uniform and collar.

'Sad news about the Imam,' Montgomery said, in a less than convincing tone.

'Yes, apparently he was a good man. Melanie seemed quite fond of him.'

'Melanie?'

'Yes, you met Melanie Underwood here, in your office.'

'Ah, yes, Melanie Underwood,' he said, glancing at his notes. 'The lady in the park! What exactly was she doing in the park with the Imam, Alan, just before he was killed?'

'She was there in an investigative capacity, Chief Superintendent.'

'I presume you are referring to the Broadwick Street murders, Alan?'

'Yes, that's correct.'

'But you have been instructed to end your enquires into that incident.'

Cornish smiled. 'I have been instructed to end the enquiries on *behalf* of the Met, Chief Superintendent.'

Montgomery twitched and moved his pen on the desk. 'So *you* are continuing to investigate the murders, is that right?'

'We are, sir.'

'And what do you hope to achieve, Alan?'

'We believe that there is going to be a terrorist attack in London in the near future, sir, and we believe it is being organised by Yara Halabi.'

Montgomery's back straightened. 'What proof do you have of this attack?'

'We have no proof, Chief Superintendent, but we believe that the target will be the "Trooping the Colour" ceremony and the terrorists intend to use Sarin, dispersed on the participants, including our *Monarch,* using commercial drones.'

Montgomery looked expectantly at Cornish as if waiting for the punchline of a joke. '...But you have no evidence *whatsoever* to support this theory?'

'No, sir.'

'And the Imam wasn't able to help you?'

'Melanie was there to ask for the Imam's assistance in finding Yara Halabi.'

'And what did he say to her?'

'He agreed to help.'

Montgomery shifted in his seat. 'And then got himself killed for the privilege!'

Cornish nodded. 'We're being watched.'

'Clearly!'

'Have your enquires turned up anything, sir?'

Montgomery sniffed uneasily. 'We are continuing to search for her but, it's fair to say, at the moment the trail is cold. Even the anti-terrorist boys are struggling. They haven't turned up any communications that would indicate that an attack is imminent, Alan, and something like you're suggesting would take a lot of organising. Especially the use of Sarin!'

Cornish sighed. 'I didn't expect you to believe me, Chief Superintendent,' he said, and began to stand up.

'Please... sit down, Alan. ...I didn't say that I don't believe you.'

Cornish raised an eyebrow.

'Yes, I know… we haven't exactly hit it off, so to speak, but I do have a lot of respect for you and your organisation and if this threat is genuine, then I would be silly to ignore your warning.'

Christ! I can't believe he just said that!

'Alan, please tell me what it is that makes you think this attack is going to happen?'

Cornish nodded pensively and replied:

'…We know that Yara Halabi got married to an ISIS fighter in Iraq and he was killed by our Special Forces not long afterwards. She ended up in Afghanistan training jihadis. Her expertise includes military drones and military weaponry, including chemical weapons. The CIA say that she's had experience of the use of Sarin in Syria and this was confirmed with Israel's military intelligence, Aman.'

'But this is all supposition isn't it?'

'Yes, but ask yourself, why would she risk coming to this country just to kill a woman who's relinquished the faith? Any home-grown fanatic could do that job. She's here for a far more important reason.'

'I must agree with you, Alan, she's taken a *huge* risk coming here. So she must be expecting a *huge* payback.'

'And no doubt she's prepared to die for her cause, too.'

'They all are, aren't they? Bloody insane, the lot of them. The trouble is, they want the rest of us dead too!' Montgomery picked up the receiver and ordered a pot of coffee.

He then continued:

'As you well know, Alan, Neil Bartholomew, for whatever reason, wanted this case closed down, but this case has moved to another level now and I need to re-open it; and we need to work together. This is about a threat to the Monarchy and I believe MI5 and the Prime Minister need to be involved.'

I can't believe I'm hearing this! This pompous bastard is actually listening to reason for once. Cornish replied:

'I must say, Chief Superintendent, I wasn't expecting to hear that from you.'

'Why is that? Did you think I was a pompous bastard, Alan?'

Cornish just smiled.

'There's no need to answer that!'

Cornish laughed. 'We're happy to work with you—again! But I'm sure you're aware, Chief Superintendent, time is of the essence,' he stressed, 'Trooping the Colour is always on the second Saturday of June.'

'Yes, I realise that, Alan,' Montgomery replied, 'so we need to talk to the Commissioner and MI5,' he said, picking up the receiver, 'because this is nothing to do with Neil Bartholomew anymore.'

The Commissioner! Christ! He is taking this seriously. Cornish realised. This wasn't the rejection he'd been expecting on his way to the Met today, but he was inwardly delighted that Montgomery had finally come to his senses and was listening to him.

Unbeknownst to Cornish and Montgomery, the Iranian registered container ship, carrying a hidden package of radio controlled detonators, had berthed safely at the London docks, and Yara Halabi was there to collect them.

Now she had the drones, the Sarin and the detonators; the three key components necessary to cause unimaginable carnage in the city of London!

Chapter 41

TEA AND CAKES

Cornish served the sizzling bacon onto Melanie's plate and then served up two perfectly cooked poached eggs. 'Do you want toast with that, my love?' he asked.

'No thanks, that looks more than enough, thank you,' she said, settling down at the breakfast table to eat. 'So what do you think has happened to change Montgomery's mind?'

Cornish slipped his breakfast plate onto the table and sat down opposite Melanie. 'I'm not really sure, love. I think the death of the Imam was significant and the fact that we'd done our homework on Yara Halabi. I certainly wasn't expecting an audience with the Commissioner when I arrived there.'

'What's he like?' Melanie asked.

'Commissioner Wilks was impressive, I must say. We went to see him to ask for his support and he listened to our arguments intently. In the end, he said that there was no evidence to support our hypothesis, and I thought, here we go

226

again. But then he said that if *we* were proven to be right and *he'd* chosen to ignore the warnings then his head would be on the chopping block—and he wasn't too keen on that idea! In his summing up he said that sometimes you have to be prepared for the unthinkable.'

'So will they now put more effort into finding Yara Halabi?'

'Precisely, along with MI5, but so will we. We have a greater flexibility than the Met and we can do things quicker, because if we've called this scenario correctly, then time is running out.'

Melanie poured steaming black coffee from a cafetière into two breakfast mugs and Cornish added a spoon of brown sugar into one of them.

'I've tried to give up sugar in my coffee but I can't do it,' he said, despondently.

'Just keep reducing the amount a bit at a time. It worked for me.'

'Okay, I'll try it.' Cornish sipped his coffee and then said:

'Darling, I think it's time you and I had a picnic in St James's Park.'

'Really! I though you said time was running out? And now all of a sudden you want to swan off to London for a *picnic*!'

'Well, I don't intend to waste time while we're there.'

'Your scheming again, aren't you?'

Cornish smiled and nodded. 'I want to do a recce. I want to look at the location and I want to try and understand how she intends to implement this attack. But more importantly I want you, as a psychologist, to get into the mind of a terrorist. We need to be one step ahead of her, not chasing our tails.'

'Shall I make some sandwiches then?'

'Let's just have tea and cakes,' Cornish replied.

*

The morning cloud had disappeared and St James's Park was now bathed in sunshine. The colourful throng of early summer tourists were enjoying the warm weather and the expanse of grass near the lake was popular with people, ducks and dragonflies alike.

Cornish and Melanie had walked through the park and were now standing with their backs to the 38 feet high, Portland Stone, Guards Memorial, looking out at the expanse of Horse Guards Parade.

'Over there,' Cornish said, 'is the Ministry of Defence Building.'

'And behind it is the River Thames and the London Eye,' Melanie added.

'Correct!' Cornish agreed.

Melanie looked all around her and occasionally checked the satellite images of the area on her iPhone. Eventually, she walked up to Cornish and said:

'In my opinion she has *two* possible options here. She could initiate the attack from the park or she could use the river to her advantage.'

Cornish nodded. 'You mean from a boat?'

'Yeah, and fly the drones over the top of the Ministry of Defence building. How ironic would that be?'

'Jesus Christ! That's just the kind of thing that audacious bitch would do.'

Melanie smiled. 'Exactly! It's easy access to the target area and well within the range of the drones.'

'And an easy escape route too, unlike the park!' Cornish added, convinced Melanie had guessed it right.

Melanie puffed out her cheeks and exhaled.

Cornish put his arm around her shoulders, kissed her on the cheek and said:

'We need to alert Montgomery and get the Marine Police involved immediately; because the River Thames is their domain. I'll get Tom Weiss to scour the waterfront boat hire as well; he's got ears like an elephant, but he's also got eyes like a bilge rat, which might come in handy down there!'

'Oh God, Alan—what if we've got this *completely* wrong? You must have considered that?'

'Yes, I have, and I know it's all supposition. But at least we've alerted the authorities to the *potential* threat, of which, remember, they were *completely* unaware! And, we've *both* come to the same conclusion about the modus operandi of the potential attack.'

Melanie managed to smile. 'That's very true, but just *one* shred of evidence would be nice, Alan,' Melanie said, as her phone rang in her pocket.

She took the call:

'Melanie Underwood speaking,' she said, and then she listened, motionless, to the nervous voice of a man who introduced himself as Hassan, the brother of the murdered Imam.

After the call, Melanie looked at Cornish and said:

'I'm afraid we don't have time for a picnic today—but we do now have a shred of evidence.'

'What kind of evidence?' Cornish asked, excitedly.

'I'll tell you on the way back, ' Melanie replied. 'Come on, we need to go!'

Chapter 42

THE VENOM OF A MILLION DEADLY SNAKES

A flat somewhere in east London

'Am I looking at the finished product?' Yara Halabi asked the man holding the drone.

'Yes—apart from the vial of course, which fits into this rubber holder next to the detonator,' he said, pointing to his handiwork. 'We have tested the detonators and they work. When we send a radio signal from this controller to the detonators they explode, smashing the vials and releasing the Sarin liquid which, at ambient temperature, will quickly turn to gas.'

'What about the range?'

'The target is well within the range of the drones. There will be no worries there. We will have clear images, from the drone's on-board cameras, on the laptop screens aboard the

231

boat and I will make sure we record everything, so that the devastation can be beamed around the world.'

Yara Halabi allowed herself a smile. 'You have done well. You have all done well. I am very pleased,' she said, and all seven men visibly relaxed. 'I presume the boat has been hired?' she asked, nonchalantly, to no-one in particular.

'The boat has been hired for two whole days and we have a skipper,' someone replied.

'What is a skipper?'

'Someone to steer the boat. Don't worry—it's one of us.'

One of the men raised his hand in acknowledgement and said:

'We will have access from nine o'clock on the Friday morning.'

Yara Halabi nodded her approval. 'Good, that will give us plenty of time to get everything ready for the greatest spectacle on Earth,' she replied. 'I want the ISIS flag to be flying as we approach the bridge and I want to stand at the front of the boat, enjoying every minute of my dream, as we sail up the river. They are ignorant of what is going to happen,' she said, 'and we are about to inflict upon the infidels, the venom of a *million* deadly snakes and they will grovel in the dust, writhing in agony and dying the death they deserve. It will be a *wondrous* moment. It will be *our* moment to wreak the long-awaited *revenge* on the enemies of Islam. *Allahu Akbar!*'

Chapter 43

MENTIONED IN DISPATCHES

Metropolitan Police Headquarters, Victoria Embankment

'This information is highly significant,' Chief Superintendent Montgomery said, after hearing Melanie explain the details of the phone call.

Melanie nodded her agreement. 'He insisted that he would not meet me in person and after what had happened to his brother, I can understand his concerns.'

'Yes, quite,' Montgomery replied. 'I have no doubt that what he was describing is liquid Sarin and to get it here in Ghee butter is bloody clever and very worrying; and it shows that these fanatics will stop at *nothing* to achieve their goals.'

Cornish replied:

'Hassan also said that the delivery of drones had been picked up from his shop and taken away some four days ago.

233

Using the shop address for deliveries meant that they couldn't be traced, but we know they're somewhere in the East End, operating under radio silence!'

'So far, it seems that you guys have guessed it right, and now you think the attack will come from the River Thames, via a boat?'

Melanie answered:

'Yes, we do. We've considered the possible options and the river appears to be the most logical. It would be easy to fly the drones from there to Horse Guards Parade.'

'Over the Ministry of Defence building!' Cornish added.

Montgomery shook his head. 'The audacity of the woman!' he exclaimed. 'Our response needs to be equally managed. We need to involve the expertise of the navy and the army and our special forces and chemical warfare experts will be needed to deal with this kind of incident. I intend to meet with the Commissioner after our meeting and he will be speaking in person to the Prime Minister later today. This information will instigate a COBRA meeting.'

'I just hope we've called this right, sir.' Cornish stressed.

'You and your organisation have been invaluable to us and your persistence is something to be admired, Alan.'

'Thank you, sir.'

'But the fact is, you can't do any more; it's up to us now.'

'It's going to be a very nervous time, waiting,' Melanie said.

Montgomery agreed and then said:

'But, Miss Underwood, if we are successful in stopping this attack, I will make sure you are mentioned in dispatches.' He then got to his feet and walked around to the front of his desk. 'Once again, thank you both for your efforts. I now need to get this operation underway so you'll have to excuse me.' Montgomery shook hands with Cornish and Melanie and then escorted them to the lifts.

'He's right, there is no more we can do. It's out of our hands now,' Cornish said, as they walked out of the Met building and headed along the Embankment towards Westminster.

'I know,' Melanie confessed, 'it's so frustrating though, to know that we can't do any more.'

'Can you imagine the weight of responsibility he must have on his shoulders at this moment in time ?'

Melanie remembered what the Imam said in the park and she repeated his words, quietly:

'What was that?'

'It was something the Imam said. *Suddenly I feel the weight of the world pressing down upon my shoulders*'

'He also said, *don't let them get away with it*,' Cornish added.

'Yes, he did, with his last breath,' Melanie replied, pensively. '…Let's hope his wish comes true.'

Arm in arm, they stopped and gazed down in silence at the flowing river; their thoughts running wild.

Melanie looked at Cornish and finally broke the silence, saying:

'You realise we're either going to be heroes or we're going to be villains in an ignominious debacle—and the wait is going to be *unbearable!*'

'That's the game we're in I'm afraid, but we need to be strong and trust our intuitions and suspicions. Just imagine if we have got it right! Life will carry on as normal. The London Eye will continue to turn, Big Ben will chime and the camera wielding tourists will be happily taking photos next to the guards outside the palace and, hoping beyond hope, for a glance of the Queen.'

'…Oh, I do hope so, Alan, because the alternative doesn't bear thinking about.'

'I want you to be mentioned in *dispatches*,' Cornish said, proudly, as they continued along the Embankment.

'I'm not quite sure what that means,' Melanie confessed, and Cornish laughed out loud. He paused and placed his hands on her shoulders. Gazing into her eyes, he said:

'That's because you're far too young, my love—and far too *beautiful*.'

'…You want that last sandwich, don't you?' Melanie teased.

'…Go on then, if you insist,' he replied

Chapter 44

TROOPING THE COLOUR

Melanie woke at seven o'clock to find she was alone in bed. Anxiety gripped her as she realised what day it was. '*Alan!*' she called out.

'I'm up on the roof!' he replied.

She found the sound of his voice so reassuring and climbed the stairs to join him. He was sitting at the table enjoying a mug of coffee and a buttered croissant.

'I couldn't sleep.'

'You're as nervous as me,' Melanie replied.

'I know.'

'Are we staying here?' Melanie asked.

'I thought we'd watch it on the TV. Tom Weiss has insisted on going there and he promised to keep me up to date with all the action.'

'I hope there won't be any action, other than marching and brass bands!'

'Yeah, so do I,' Cornish replied.

'How can you eat? My stomach is churning.'

'No breakfast for you then?'

'Definitely not! I'm going for a shower and then I think I'll go for a long walk along the river. Do you fancy coming with me?'

'Yeah, why not. It's going to be a long morning otherwise.'

*

Cornish switched on the TV as the broadcast started. Horse Guards Parade was bathed in sunshine and the cameras panned the seven thousand, excited, flag-waving spectators and dignitaries, seated around the parade ground, watching excitedly as the perfectly straight lines of red and black uniformed soldiers formed moving, changing patterns with typical British military precision. Moves that had been rehearsed for weeks to the familiar, marching music of the army's brass bands.

Lining the Mall, almost two hundred Welsh Guards awaited the arrival of Her Majesty the Queen, who would soon be driven from Buckingham Palace to Horse Guards Parade to enjoy the annual Queen's Birthday Parade.

Melanie was a nervous wreck and found it hard to sit down for more than a few moments at a time; but her third glass of white wine seemed to be helping.

'Beer,' she said, handing Cornish a bottle of cold Moretti, as the sound of the British Grenadiers pounded out of the Bose speaker behind the TV. They watched as the synchronised, moving matrix of Red and Black seemed to almost levitate across the parade ground

'Thanks, love,' he said. 'How are you feeling?'

'I'm a nervous fucking wreck, to be honest, Alan.'

'So am I, if it's any consolation,' Cornish replied. 'The escort has received the colour and now they're about to commence the slow march.'

'Where's the Queen?' Melanie asked.

'She's under a small canopy on the saluting base, with the Duke of Kent, watching the proceedings.'

'Oh God, this is turning my hair grey,' Melanie said, filling her wine glass again.

Cornish sipped his beer and said:

'Okay, so the trooping is officially done. Now we have the march past. That's where the troops parade right in front of the Queen.'

'This is it, isn't it?'

'If it's going to happen—yes, this is it,' Cornish replied, as his mobile started ringing on the table. Melanie picked it up and quickly handed it to him.

'It's Tom,' he said, and answered the call in speaker mode so that Melanie could hear the conversation. 'Tom—so far so good,' he said, 'it's all going to plan on the parade, I'm glad to say.'

'It might be on the parade, Alan, but it *fucking* crazy here!'

'Where are you?'

'I'm standing on Westminster Bridge watching the action.'

'What's happening, Tom?'

'The boat sailed up the river a few minutes ago, flying the ISIS flag. A woman dressed in a black burka, I presume it was Yara Halabi, was standing at the front of boat. When they neared the bridge the boat stopped and a number of men emerged holding drones. The woman called out something in Arabic and the men raised the drones ready to launch. But then, there was a number of dull explosions on both sides of the boat's hull, which really rocked the boat, throwing two of them into the water, and within seconds it was sinking, fast. None of the drones were launched. Yara Halabi appeared to panic and it looked like she was trying to explode her suicide vest, but soon she was flailing about in the water, shouting something in Arabic. I was close enough to see the fear in her eyes, Alan. Robbed of her glorious death, and in less than a minute, the river had taken her. It was the cold water of the Thames that filled her lungs and finally silenced her *evil* rhetoric.'

'That's fantastic news, Tom,' Cornish enthused.

'It was all planned to the second, Alan—a covert counter operation. There are police and military divers everywhere now, looking for the crew, but there doesn't seem to be any sign of them, as yet. I don't think any of them could swim.'

Cornish jumped up, punched the air, and yelled:

'We did it! We *fucking* did it, Mel!'

Melanie burst into tears of joy.

On the TV, the Queen smiled her approval as the massed guards marched past, saluting their Monarch.

There were smiles too from the Defence Secretary, the Prime Minister and Commissioner Wilks, sitting in the stands, clearly enjoying the spectacle.

Chapter 45

AN ASSASSIN IN WENCESLAS SQUARE

One week later

'I have to do this—I need to confirm my suspicions,' Cornish said, 'and it's an excuse for us to have a few days in Prague on company expenses.'

'I've never been to Prague,' Melanie said, clearly warming to the idea. 'So what are you hoping to achieve by going there.'

'I'm looking for some answers and the only person who can help me is Tomas Soukal.'

'The assassin?!'

'Yes, but don't worry, he's not going to shoot you.'

'How are you going to find him?'

'I already have a meeting set up with him in Prague this Friday. After that, we can enjoy the rest of the weekend exploring the city.'

'Is he expecting you to hire him or something?'

'No nothing like that, although I did have a hare-brained idea like that, but Tom Weiss didn't seem too keen on it.'

'So when do we fly?' Melanie asked.

'Friday morning,' Cornish replied, 'we meet up with Tomas Soukal at five p.m., in Wenceslas Square.'

'Sounds romantic, except for the fact that he's a cold-blooded murderer!'

'You don't need to meet him. You can always go shopping and I'll catch up with you later.'

'I'm not sure. I'll think about it,' she said, teased by the thought of being face-to-face with a professional assassin. 'So, what are you going to ask him?'

'You'll have to wait, I'm afraid. A man is allowed a few secrets you know.'

'Alan—don't tease!'

*

The rain had stopped and the evening was very humid. Wenceslas Square, in Prague, was busy with shoppers and people eating and drinking at the many street restaurants.

Tomas Soukal was sitting at a table at the far end of the square, overlooked by the National Museum. He was sipping a strong, espresso coffee and smoking a cigarette. His eyes darted from side to side as he watched the crowds passing by. It was a good place to meet a stranger. It was noisy, very public and easy to escape into the mass of people—if it became necessary to do so.

He sipped his espresso and, as he stubbed out his cigarette butt in the ashtray a voice said:

'Tomas Soukal?'

He looked up to see Alan Cornish and Melanie Underwood standing next to his table.

'I'm Alan Cornish and this is my partner, Melanie. May we join you?' Cornish asked.

'Be my guests,' he said.

Cornish and Melanie settled at the table and Tomas Soukal called the waiter over. 'Coffee?' he asked.

'Well, we're sort of celebrating this weekend, so we'd like a Czech beer, if that's okay?'

'Will you let me choose for you?'

'Of course,' Cornish replied.

'Dvě plzně, prosím,' Tomas Soukal instructed the waiter.

For a moment there was a pregnant pause before Cornish spoke:

'We appreciate you agreeing to see us,' he said.

'What are you celebrating?' the assassin asked.

Cornish looked at Melanie and smiled. 'We helped to stop an assassination attempt.'

'Are you trying to put me out of business?' the young assassin asked.

'All of the time,' Cornish replied, and waited for the response. Thankfully Tomas Soukal laughed, which helped to release some of tension all three were feeling.

The waiter arrived with the two beers and placed them on the table.

'Enjoy,' Soukal said, smiling at Melanie.

Very handsome—for a cold-blooded psychopath, she thought.

Cornish and Melanie then sipped their beers.

'That's good,' Cornish said.

'Very good,' Melanie agreed.

'So—what have you come all of this way for if it's not to arrest me, Mr Cornish?'

'Clearly, I don't have any evidence to arrest you—but if I did, then I would.'

'Assuming you could catch me!'

'Yes, of course, and I don't underestimate the difficulty of that. But you trusted me, and I appreciate that. I won't be chasing you around Europe, rest assured, Tomas. I'll leave that to Interpol.'

Soukal laughed. 'Most generous of you, Mr Cornish. So what is it you want from me?'

Cornish took out a photograph from his breast pocket and passed it over to Soukal.

'Is that the man who funded your job in London?'

Melanie's mouth opened in surprise.

Soukal looked at the photo and said:

'Why should I tell *you*? I never reveal my clients. I'm sure you can appreciate that?'

Cornish nodded his agreement and replied:

'But, as you well know, Tomas, being Czech, freedom and democracy don't come easy. Sadly, they often have to be fought for and people give their lives in the belief that freedom is worth fighting for. We in the UK are under constant threat from dangerous ideologies. Russia is no friend of ours and Putin would love our capitalist economy to collapse. And the same applies to your country too. I'm sure your generation wouldn't welcome the sight of Russian tanks trundling around this beautiful square again, would they?'

'That's true, we enjoy our freedom now, and we hate the Russians for what they did to our country,' he said.

Cornish smiled. 'Surprisingly, it seems that we have some common interests, Tomas?'

Tomas Soukal glanced at the photo again and said:

'…Yeah that's him, he's a Russian sympathiser; he's been working for the Russians for years.'

'I thought so,' Cornish said. 'Did he fund the killing of Maksim Mikhailov?'

Soukal handed the photograph back to Cornish and said:

'Yes, it was him.'

Cornish handed the photo to Melanie, who stared at the familiar face in disbelief.

Chapter 46

THE INVITATION

Metropolitan Police Headquarters, Victoria Embankment

Chief Superintendent Montgomery shook hands warmly, with Cornish and Melanie. 'The whole operation was a complete success thanks to Probe, Alan. Please take a seat, both,' he said, 'coffee and biscuits are on the way.'

'Apparently it was a very impressive operation, Chief Superintendent, according to our man Tom Weiss, who had a ringside seat on Westminster Bridge.'

'Is he the guy who alerted us to the boat they used?'

'Yes, that's him.'

Montgomery smiled and said:

'I must admit, "Operation Waterfront" was impressive. The area around Westminster Bridge and the London Eye had been evacuated by the police, and strategically populated with military personnel dressed in civvies. We even had a few buses

248

and a white van crossing the bridge. So, to the terrorists, everything must have appeared normal. The army had two Sarin antidote stations, disguised as portable blood donor units, down by the riverbank—but thankfully, they weren't needed. During the night, Navy divers planted four, small, limpet mines to the bottom of the boat, which exploded, on cue, with military precision. The boat sank in less than thirty-seconds! All of the drones were recovered and only two of the vials had broken, but apparently, according to the army ops team, they broke under water, so they were not considered a health risk to the public. Four bodies have so far been recovered from the river and I can confirm that one of them was that of Yara Halabi. She was wearing a suicide vest! She must have sunk like a stone!'

Cornish replied:

'Clearly, she had no intention of getting wet! Will there be a press release, sir?'

'Yes, but she won't get a mention.'

Melanie then said:

'I'm sure her suicide vest was heavy—but it wasn't as heavy as the hatred in her heart!'

'This country never ceases to amaze me, Melanie. We always seem to come through in the face of adversity. But that doesn't mean we can take our foot off the pedal, because, there will always be people in this world who want to crush freedom and democracy.'

'Like a certain man from MI6,' Cornish replied.

'Yes, that *bastard*!'

'When he found out I was going to Prague, he must have realised I was on to him.'

'He'd already destroyed all of the copies of Mikhailov's top secret information. Thanks to your call from Prague, we detained him at the airport; the rat was on his way to Moscow. You'll be pleased to know that he's going to be tried for high treason, which carries a life sentence, so we'll need you in court, Alan.'

'I'll be happy to help, sir.'

'They hanged traitors like him years ago… I'm sure Russia must have paid Neil Bartholomew a *fortune* to prevent that information getting into *enemy* hands.'

Cornish nodded and replied:

'If it's any consolation, sir, we were hacked as well. Zeezee is *mortified*, and I'm not sure if he'll ever get over it! But the one thing ZeeZee does religiously, is back-up his work.' With that Cornish removed a USB stick from his top pocket. 'It's all on there, sir,' he said, handing it to Montgomery.

Montgomery shook his head in disbelief. 'Alan Cornish, you and your team are national treasures. Thank you.'

Cornish smiled with pride and winked at Melanie. 'It appears that our *extortionate* rates turned out to be good value for money in the end, Chief Superintendent!'

Montgomery smirked and nodded in agreement. 'Rest assured, this is one bill I'll be happy to pay, Alan.'

After finishing their coffee and biscuits, Montgomery walked to the lifts with his visitors and shook their hands as the doors of the lift opened

'No offence, Alan, but let's hope I never need your services again,' he said, jovially.

'Well, if you do, you know where to find us, sir.'

Montgomery nodded and said:

'I certainly do, my friend….Oh, by the way, I nearly forgot to tell you that there's a letter on its way to you, inviting you both to a party.'

'How nice—I love a good party,' Melanie said, excitedly. 'It looks like we might be visiting a dress shop, or two, tomorrow, Alan.'

Cornish rolled his eyes and tutted. '…And where's the party to, sir?' he asked.

'Ohhh, don't get *too* excited Alan—it's only a small party, for a few—*special* people.'

'Here in London, sir?'

'Yes, at Buckingham Palace!' he replied, coolly. 'I look forward to seeing you both there, in far more—convivial circumstances.' Montgomery smiled broadly and winked, and as the lift doors began to close, he turned and walked away, with his shoulders back and a bounce in his step.

Cornish and Melanie stood speechless as the lift descended and a tear trickled down Melanie's face as she struggled to control her emotions.

Cornish reached out and gently wiped the tear away with his finger. 'You must have been mentioned in dispatches,' he said, proudly.

'I can't believe that this is actually happening. It's like being in a dream... And do you know what the icing on the cake is for me?'

'What?'

'I kept my promise to the Imam,' she said, proudly, as her eyes welled up.

Cornish wrapped his arms around her and held her tight.

'Yes, you did,' he replied. 'The good man didn't die in vain.'

'No, he didn't,' Melanie replied, and promptly burst into a flood of emotional tears.

Thirty minutes later they'd checked into the Waldorf Hotel and were taking a power shower together.

'I've got a lot of tension in my body,' Melanie said, as she rinsed her hair.

Cornish pulled her close and kissed her. 'It won't be there for much longer,' he said, and carried her, wet and naked, into the bedroom.

THE END

Thank you for reading RETRIBUTION. I hope you enjoyed the story as much as I did writing it.

Other books by Harry Waterman include:
Shroud the Truth With Silence

For details of all the books that I have written, please visit my website at:

haydnjones-author.com

Printed in Great Britain
by Amazon